T0385169

Jane Godwin

WHEN RAIN TURNS TO SNOW

LOTHIAN

A Lothian Children's Book

Published in Australia and New Zealand in 2020
by Hachette Australia
(an imprint of Hachette Australia Pty Limited)
Level 17, 207 Kent Street, Sydney NSW 2000
www.hachettechildrens.com.au

10 9 8 7 6 5 4 3 2

A catalogue record for this book is available from the National Library of Australia

NATIONAL LIBRARY OF AUSTRALIA

ISBN: 978 0 7344 2005 3

Cover design by Allison Colpoys
Author photo: Lillie Thompson
Typeset in 11.2/16 pt Minion Pro by Bookhouse, Sydney
Printed and bound in Great Britain by Clays Ltd, Elcograf S.p.A.

MIX
Paper from responsible sources
FSC® C001695

The paper this book is printed on is certified against the Forest Stewardship Council® Standards. McPherson's Printing Group holds FSC® chain of custody certification SA-COC-005379. FSC® promotes environmentally responsible, socially beneficial and economically viable management of the world's forests.

For Caroline, Paddy, and Bruce Springsteen

REED

My favourite word is sandal. It feels so open, so clear and simple, it makes me think of a little kid in summer.

A little kid – maybe it's a memory, maybe it's me – now skipping along, now balancing on that bit of concrete at the edge of the gutter.

Wearing

Sandals.

Flat – are they red? – with shiny buckles.

I like the way the word looks. With the two a's like that. And you can make it sound really slow in your mouth.

Not like paddock. Sadie's favourite word is paddock. It's nice to say, but it's a closed, clipped word, like the locking of a gate. You can't linger on paddock like you can on sandal.

Hana's favourite word is serendipity. The slow, sliding 'seren' and then the quick tongue-on-the-roof-of-your-mouth 'dipity'. Satisfying.

And reed. The name for tall plants that grow beside a dam or a lake somewhere. Or a creek. A reed can also be part of a musical instrument, an oboe or clarinet. But Reed can be a name, too. I thought when he told me his name, he was telling me to read. Like, to read something. Of course I didn't see how it's spelt when he said it out loud that day. And I thought, Read what? But it's like this: Reed.

I like that word, too. It's got a long sound in the middle but a definite ending. Definite, but not defiant like paddock.

Sometimes I make a list of words. Of things to say, or just what I'm thinking. I can never think of the best thing to say when I'm in the middle of a conversation. Like when Amber gave everyone but me a piece of chewy, and I said that wasn't very nice, she's like, 'Don't make such a big deal of it, Lissa, it's only a piece of chewy.' I said, 'I'm not making a big deal of it,' and she smiled and said, 'Well look at you, you're almost crying.'

What I should have said was, 'I'm not upset about a piece of chewing gum, I'm upset because this is another small example of how you're a total B to me every day.'

You know what they call that? The wit of the staircase. It's like you think of the best thing to say when you're walking back down the staircase after an argument.

I always have that.

The wit of the staircase.

And sometimes, I have no words at all.

That was how it was when I met Reed.

Eliot says to me, 'Here, have Mercy.'
So I hold her.
And then I have to take her.

TUESDAY

1

MIST

That's a short word, but you can rest for a while on the 's' part. You can actually say that word for as long as you like.

Mist is a homophone, like reed – when the sound of the word has two meanings, but you spell it differently. Mist can also be missed. Like someone is missed, or missing.

So after dinner on Monday night, I'm putting rubbish in the bin around the side of our house, and I can just make out a shape, like a sheet covering something, up against the heating outlet under the old wooden awning. It's pretty dark, and the light around the side hasn't come on because it needs a new globe and that's the stuff Dad used to do. I know that's sexist and everything, but I'm stating a fact. Dad changed the light globes in our house. Dad mowed the lawn. Sure, he did cleaning and stuff, and he read to me when I was little. And Mum did gardening too, she just never mowed the lawn. But now she does.

Anyway, often there's stuff around the side – firewood, bags of compost, stakes for the garden up against the house like leaning wooden soldiers. But this shape seems bigger, bulkier. Maybe Mum's bought something and she's hiding it from us. But it isn't anyone's birthday, and nowhere near Christmas. It's like the middle of June. And why hide it here?

It's misty and cold, I can feel water in the air, and I want to get back inside. I only see the shape out of the corner of my eye. I don't even think about it much.

The next morning, it's *really* cold, there's fog suspended everywhere so that the Dandenongs have disappeared. Sometimes it's so clear you can almost make out the individual trees on the mountain range, and sometimes it's a still, blue mass, like a painting. But this morning it's a filmy grey sheet and if I didn't know differently, anything could be at the horizon, not mountains at all. There's frost on the grass and I know the car windscreen will have ice on it and the wipers will make that scratching sound when Mum turns them on.

When I leave for school, I go around the side. The air's so cold it makes my eyes water. Steam is coming out of the vent at the heating outlet. Have you ever noticed that? When the heating's on inside, the unit lets out warm air from a vent outside, like a kettle boiling, or when you breathe out steam on a cold morning. But the lump that had been against the heating outlet the night before isn't there anymore.

Gone.

I wonder about telling Sadie when I get to school. But she's talking with Amber and the others, who are all rubbing their hands together in the pink fingerless gloves that they bought online at the same time. And I haven't made a list, so I don't say anything. If I did say something, Amber would probably say some mean thing back. But of course I can't even think of what it would be. That's why I have the wit of the staircase, I can never think of what she'll say next.

I stand near them, stamping my feet and hugging myself against the cold.

I used to think that Amber let me hang around them because she likes my brother, Harry. Harry's in Year Eleven, he'd never be interested in her. But she always says, 'I'm like my mum, I go for older guys. Guys our age are so immature.' Amber does look older than she is, especially when we go out, because she wears her mum's shoes, and heaps of make-up.

Harry is good looking, I can see it. And he's muscly and strong because he plays footy. But he's never had a girlfriend, as far as I know. He's more into sport and he's also pretty clever so he studies quite a bit. Lots of girls like him, they're always telling me.

Amber will only come over to mine if she thinks Harry will be there. She used to talk about Harry all the time, but lately she seems to have stopped that. Thank god. It's embarrassing.

It was much better last year when Hana was here. She was, well, she still is, my best friend. In March, she moved back to Western Australia with her family. Mum used to tell me to branch out, have more friends. Maybe Mum knew that Hana would be moving one day. Her parents work in the mining industry and they come from WA. But Mum never said outright, Hana's family will be moving back to WA next year. When I told Mum, she said, 'Oh, really' but I got the feeling that she already knew. Her face didn't change, her eyes didn't do that dancing thing that happens when you're actually surprised.

Hana likes words, same as me. That was our thing. We'd do the cryptic crosswords together. And the quick. And the target words. And sometimes the sudoku, although Harry or Mum usually had to help us with that.

A word that Hana taught me is kvetching. It means to complain loudly. Like, Harry is kvetching that there are never any bananas left. Hana hardly ever complains herself, but sometimes she says to people, 'Stop your kvetching!' And even if they don't know what it means, they usually shut up. Hana could handle the girls in our year much better than I can. She didn't really care what they said or did or thought.

Sadie's being nice to me today. We sit together at lunchtime, and after school we get on the train first and then when the other Year Eights get on, she doesn't go and sit with them like she sometimes does. I wonder why she stays with me today, but not yesterday and maybe not tomorrow. When I get off, I see her go over to them. Sadie likes it that I live close to the school, and closer to the city than she does. She can stay at my place if we're all going out somewhere, unless Amber invites her to stay at hers.

I walk home quickly from the station because it's still so cold. You know those days when it never warms up at all? It's not even four-thirty, but the sun's already going down and the cars have their headlights on. It's smoggy, and still. Smog makes such a soft light in the afternoon. Like a weak sunset.

Sometimes the smog worries me, makes me think of climate change, and that maybe in the future days will always look like this. Like in China, there's terrible smog. My dad lives in China, in Beijing, but he says some days it's clear, some days the sky is as blue as when he was a kid growing up in the country back here.

Mum works till six or seven most nights at Move Australia. It's a physio and Pilates studio. They have classes there, and there's a hydrotherapy pool, and they see patients. The pool is so warm, Mum lets me go in it sometimes. I went there quite a bit after school when Hana first moved. Warm water makes everything feel better. When does a warm bath not feel good?

I'm just thinking that I might read my book for English in a warm bath as I reach the gate at the top of our driveway.

The lump is back. Is there an animal under the blanket?

I open the gate quietly, lifting the latch so that it doesn't click. I leave it open so it won't make a noise. I get closer, creeping down the side of the house.

The lump doesn't move.

I bend down to look.

Someone is in the blanket, asleep under the awning on our driveway.

I can't see who it is, or even if it's male or female, adult or child. Only a hoodie and a bit of face. I tiptoe straight past the sleeping person, up the three steps to the deck and the back door. My fingers feel frozen and I fumble to get my key from my wallet. I slide the glass door open, then lock it as soon as I get inside. I don't turn the light on, even though it's quite dark. Should I call the police? That might be over-reacting. My heart's beating fast. I stand very still and look out into our back garden. Bare trees, yellowing lawn. My hammock, wet from the rain, hanging heavy to the grass. I don't want whoever is sleeping to wake up because then what will I do? Maybe it's a homeless person. How cold must it be for those poor people in winter?

I pace around the house, put the heater on, return to the back room. It's all glass out to the deck so I can see if anyone has entered the garden. No one there. In the last shaft of sunlight that cuts across the wooden floor, I see dust on Mum's wooden owls and on the photo frames with pictures of me and Harry when we were little. I decide to call Mum. We're only supposed to call her at work if it's an emergency, but I figure this is an emergency. I speed-dial Mum. Her phone rings. And rings. And rings. She has it set to ring forever before it goes to message bank. *Hello, you've called Fiona Freeman. Leave me a message, and I'll –*

There's a noise outside, on the steps, something moves.

I turn around.

He's standing on the deck.

A kid, maybe my age, or a bit younger. Thirteen? It's hard to tell because that grey hoodie is pulled down over his face. He wears round glasses, with thin steel frames.

There's only the sliding glass door between us. The blanket's in a bundle on the outdoor table behind him, and a backpack.

'What do you want?' I call. My voice trembles, croaky.

He's still, staring.

I hold up my phone. 'I'm calling my mum, now.'

His eyes crunch up, like he's worried, or even scared, like me.

'Then I'm calling the police.' Is he a burglar? Does he have a knife? If Mum were here she'd definitely call the police. I wish

Harry was here, but he's at footy training till seven. And I'm not sure he'd be any help, actually. What would Hana do?

My phone pings. I jump. I feel as if I have to keep looking at him because this will stop him from coming closer. 'What do you want?' I say again through the glass. I'm glad I locked that door. 'You can't come in. Go away! Go home!'

He turns to go. Oh thank god. He's leaving.

I look at Mum's text.

> Did you call me? Got a client in 5. Having a quick
> drink with Troy after work. Home by 8. Soup in
> fridge you can heat up for dinner. Love you xxx

But Mum and I always have dinner together . . .

Hang on, he's not going, he's getting something from the blanket. His hood falls from his head like he's a monk, or someone from *Lord of the Rings*. I can see that he has a number two haircut, like in the army. He's quite small. Could I fight him? I don't think so, because I'm small too, for my age. He leans over into the bundle. What's he getting? A rock? A knife? A gun? I grip my phone. 'I'm going to –'

There's a noise – like a little animal or something, a little cry.

What's he got?

The kid turns around.

He's holding a baby.

His place makes me feel nervous. People half asleep on the stairs. And his room's like a cupboard. He can't even fit a proper bed there but he's still proud of it.

There's incense burning beside the mattress. Incense doesn't make me calm, it makes me think a fire might start. And I know that sometimes their friend Cathy takes some bad drug and they have to take her up to the clinic or call the ambulance.

2

FLEETING

The baby is squirming in his arms. I think it's a girl. She has hardly any hair but she's wearing a pink towelling onesie. He's holding her around her middle, out in front, like she's some bulky item that's hard to carry. Her little legs are kicking. She's lost a sock.

I try to think of the right thing to do, to say.

'Put down any weapons.' It comes out weak, as if I'm reading a line from a play, even though I'm trying to be assertive.

He shakes his head. I mean, he's holding a baby.

Finally, he speaks. 'I'm not going to hurt anyone. Sorry to frighten you, but I'm wondering if you can . . .' He pauses as if he's not quite sure what I can do. '. . . help.'

He's definitely a kid, his voice hasn't even really broken.

'Can you open the door?' he says. 'Please open the door.'

'I'm not opening it. What do you want?'

He keeps standing there, with the baby, looking helpless.

I keep standing there, too. Me on one side of the door, him on the other. A stand-off.

'Does Fiona Freeman live here?' he asks.

I'm shocked. 'How did you know that?'

He nods. 'That's what I thought.'

I open the sliding door a little. He steps towards me.

'Don't come in! Stand there,' I say.

He freezes, like it's musical statues.

'Do you know her?' I ask him. 'My mother?'

The baby is wriggling. The pale pink onesie is dirty.

He shakes his head.

'I'm her daughter Lissa,' I stammer. 'Lissa Freeman.' Should I have told him my name? Was that a bad thing to do?

'Reed.'

'Read what?'

'My name. Reed Lister.'

Lister. Sounds like my name, Lissa.

Listen, glisten, Lister, Lissa.

Sadie would say he's a nerdy-looking guy. The hoodie's way too big for him. He's wearing jeans and new-looking runners. Dirty but neat, it's dirt like a well-cared-for kid who's been on school camp, dirt you could easily wash off with soap and warm water, not like you see on the faces of people in the city sitting on the footpath with nowhere to go. And he's a teenager, I can tell from his arms and his jaw, but he's little. Like a little man.

He's hitching the baby up a bit, holding her with only one arm now. She's kind of dangling. Babies are usually clean and smell like talcum powder. Her face is quite pale, almost grey.

'Do you need to see my mother? Like, do you need a physio or something?' Mum sees mostly adults but sometimes she sees kids with sporting injuries. ACLs, back injuries from rowing, hip flexors, rotator cuffs, rolled ankles. Occasionally patients come to our house, but hardly ever. And Mum would have told me, wouldn't she?

He shakes his head. His glasses are fogging up. The steel rims are silver, like a man's glasses. He looks damp. The baby does too. The watery air has settled on them like dew. Mist. That's probably bad for a baby. She should have a beanie or something, to keep her little head warm.

'Do you need help?' I ask.

He says nothing, rubs an eye, his glasses go crooked.

'You're going to have to tell me what you need.'

He just says, 'I've come a long way.' He looks exhausted, like he almost might cry, and the baby, too. She's still wriggling around, as if she's uncomfortable but can't work out where. He opens his eyes wide. They're a grey/green colour, it's like his eyes are asking me a question, wanting something from me. Expecting something.

I want him to leave me alone, leave my house. But there's something about him, and I can't yell at him to go. He looks as if he needs more than one kind of help. All I can think of to say is, 'Do you need some food?'

He nods.

'Stay there.' I close the door and lock it, go over to the kitchen bench, pick up an apple and the last banana from the fruit bowl. I have to put the fruit on the floor so I can unlock the door again. I hold them out to him.

'Thanks.' He reaches with his hand but as he's holding the baby too, he can't take both the banana and the apple, so

13

I have to go outside and put them on the table, as if he's an animal and I'm leaving snacks out for him. I rush back inside, our eyes meet for a second, but I'm keeping my distance from him and the baby.

He settles himself at the table with the baby on his knee and peels the banana.

I stand at the door, open it a bit more.

The baby is totally staring at the banana.

'Does the baby need anything?' I ask.

'I don't know.'

He eats the banana in hungry gulps. 'Do you have any water?'

I pour him a glass of water. It's straight from the tap but it's as cold as water from the fridge.

'Thank you.' Then he says, 'Do you have, like, a sandwich?'

Who am I, his personal waitress? I suppose I have to make him a sandwich. 'Vegemite, or peanut butter?'

His eyes light up as if he's a little kid and I've offered him one of those big circular lollipops. 'Peanut butter, please.'

I make the sandwich and bring it over to the door. The air's freezing out there, and now it's starting to rain. 'Take that with you and go,' I say.

The baby lets out a little cough. It sounds like the beginning of a big cough but it stops. Our deck doesn't have a roof, only an umbrella over the table, and it feels silly to put that up. 'I'm getting wet out here,' he says anxiously. He's got those eyes that go down at the corners. 'We're both getting wet. Please, can we come inside?'

What can I do? Leave him and the baby out there in the rain?

I open the door, and in he comes. With his bag, and the baby. 'Only for a minute,' I add. 'Till the rain stops.' I leave the door open a bit.

'Thanks. Is anyone else here?' he asks, his eyes darting around.

'Only me,' I say.

'Is anyone going to come home soon?'

'No.' Oh god, I shouldn't have told him that! 'My mum could, um, actually be home any minute.' I don't think he believes me.

I pick up the blanket. It's heavy and damp and smells like a wet dog. I drop it over the heating vent on the floor.

I put the plate with the sandwich on the table. 'You can't stay here. As soon as the rain stops, you need to go. Where do you live?'

'Ballarat.'

Ballarat? It's like an hour and a half away by car, up the Western Freeway. 'Have you run away from home?'

He sits down, which makes me feel nervous, like he intends to stay. 'Not really. Kind of. Maybe.'

What sort of answer is that? 'How did you get here?'

'Train.'

'All the way from –'

'Ballarat, yes.'

'That's a long way. With a baby and everything. Is she your sister?'

He shakes his head, munching through the sandwich and finishing the first half in like thirty seconds. Maybe I should have made him two sandwiches.

He looks way too young for the baby to be his, but I know that people do sometimes have kids when they're really young. Like fourteen or fifteen.

'Is she your baby?'

'Technically, no. But I'm caring for her . . .' He says this with confidence, as if he's an adult and I should think it's all totally normal. '. . . for the time being.'

'What's her name?'

He looks down at her and his little businessman face softens. 'Mercy.'

'How old is she?'

'She's, um,' Reed looks up, calculating in his head, 'almost five months.'

I hold my hand to her. 'Hi, Mercy.' She wraps her fingers around one of mine. It makes me smile, just for a second. She has tiny, dirty fingernails. Then she coughs again and he says, 'Oh, Mercy, it's okay,' and lifts her up against his shoulder, patting her back.

This time, the cough sounds like an adult cough coming from a baby. It's loud, and all the way down in her chest, in her body somewhere.

'I don't get how you know my mother's name,' I say. 'What are you doing here?' He is really strange, this whole thing is strange.

He doesn't answer me, just hoovers the rest of the peanut-butter sandwich and gulps down a bit more water and jiggles Mercy.

I think he's about to answer my question, when Mercy starts to grizzle. He sighs, agitated, his hoodie falls down over his glasses, he rocks the baby up and down and looks at me as if I'm going to know what to do. 'Do you have any food for babies?'

'I don't know what babies eat. Don't they drink from a bottle?'

'Oh yeah, hang on. Um, can you hold her?' He hops up. 'Be careful.'

I don't really have a choice because he's already holding the baby out to me. I put out my arms and he places Mercy into them.

I can't remember holding a baby before. She's a nice weight in my arms. I feel a vibration in her chest as she breathes in and out. She's wheezy, as my mum would say. She's very warm.

My phone pings and I ignore it, but I wonder if it's Mum texting again.

I look closely at Mercy. A miniature human. Soft cheeks, fine hair, tiny eyelashes. Her cheeks are red now. Her little ears are red, too. I touch them. They're hot. She stares right at me, as if she's studying me. Her eyes are glassy blue, like a swimming pool on a sunny day.

Reed pulls out an empty baby's bottle from his backpack on the floor. 'Have you got any milk?'

'Okay, I can give you some milk, but then you need to take your baby and go home. Back to Ballarat. I think she has a temperature. Look, she's quite hot. She needs her mum or dad. Have you got a myki? For the train?'

He shakes his head in little panicky bursts, the bottle's trembling in his hand.

'I can't go home,' he says.

'Why not?'

'Your mother –'

Someone's coming up the steps to the deck. I hand Mercy back.

'Hey, I've been messaging you, why don't you look at your phone? Mum's waiting in the car. I need to get –'

'Oh, hi.' It's Sadie. She pulls the sliding door across and steps inside. Reed's standing there with Mercy in his arms.

She turns to me. 'Who's that? And that?' She points to Mercy.

'Mercy,' I say. 'And Reed. He was, um, in the driveway.'

'Hi,' says Reed, holding the bottle in one hand and extending his other hand to Sadie as if this is some kind of job interview.

Sadie ignores Reed and his hand. 'Do you know each other?'

'No, we're, um, just working out why Reed is here.'

Reed goes over and opens the fridge. 'I don't think you've got any milk.'

'Lissa,' says Sadie, 'can you come outside for a minute?'

I follow Sadie outside. It's still raining so we huddle under the eave. Rain splatters in on us.

'Who is that guy?'

'He was just here, in the driveway!'

'What's he doing here?'

'I don't know. He might have run away.'

'Have you called the police?'

I shake my head.

Sadie makes a noise with her mouth like a click and a sigh. There's not really a word for it, or I can't find one. She does it after almost everything I say. Sometimes it goes with eye-rolling. I don't want to call the police. I don't think he's dangerous. I know he's got a baby and everything but I don't want to do the wrong thing by him. And he seems to know my

18

mother. Her name, anyway, he must have got her name from somewhere. And our address.

Sadie reaches for her phone. 'Don't,' I say. 'I'll find out what he's doing here first.' I don't want Sadie to get him in trouble. I don't know why, but I think he needs someone to protect him.

Reed is coming out to the deck. 'Please don't tell anyone I'm here, just yet.'

'Stay there!' Sadie shouts at him, and Mercy gets a fright. She startles in Reed's arms, and she begins to cry. Reed takes her back inside.

A car horn sounds. 'That's Mum,' says Sadie. 'I came to get the history homework coz I left mine at school.'

'I've already done half of it. On the weekend.'

'Great. Can I take a photo? I won't copy, I'll do my own answers.'

Sadie often does this. It's annoying. History's my favourite subject, and I've put heaps of thought into my answers.

She follows me inside. I get the homework from my bag on the bench.

Reed is sitting at the table with Mercy, feeding her from the bottle. 'I couldn't find milk,' he says, 'so I'm giving her water.' He's cradling her head in his arm as she drinks, spilling some down the side of her little chin.

'Is that water sterilised?' Sadie asks him.

'What?'

'Did you boil it?'

'It's from the tap.'

'You can't give babies water like that. You have to boil it.'

'Wouldn't that be too hot for them?'

'Of course it would! You boil it, then you wait for it to cool!' Sadie does her sigh, rolls her eyes.

'Here's the stuff for history,' I say. 'I could just email you the questions –' but Sadie's already put my iPad on the table and is photographing each section of the questions, and my answers, on the Vietnam War. Her mum is beeping the horn out on the street.

'Come outside again with me,' she says.

Reed struggles to his feet, still feeding the baby.

'Not you,' says Sadie, 'her.'

I walk Sadie quickly back up the driveway. The rain is getting harder.

'He might try to rob you.'

'I don't think he'd do that. He seems pretty, I don't know, young.'

'You can never tell. You know about the Melbourne crime gangs?'

'Sadie, I don't think he's in a crime gang. He has a baby with him.'

'He could have stolen the baby. Just my personal opinion. I mean, he's got no idea what to give her to drink.'

'I'll wait till Mum or Harry get home, they'll know what to do. I wish he'd go, but I don't think he's like, dangerous or anything.'

'All I'm saying is that he could be faking. Anyway, I can't wait with you, I've got maths coaching. Just get rid of him.'

She marches off, then calls from the top of the driveway. 'Send me updates.'

Updates? 'Sadie, don't tell anyone, okay?'

Sadie's mum waves from the car. 'Hurry up, get out of the rain, we'll be late!'

'And don't tell your mum,' I add, but I don't think Sadie hears me.

I always feel that Sadie's mum doesn't really like me, that I'm not good enough to be a friend of Sadie's, or that she wants more successful or popular girls, from the originals, to be friends with her daughter. The originals are the ones who've been at the school since prep. I only came in Year Seven. Which makes me not an original. Hana wasn't an original. Sadie isn't one either, but she pretends to be. Amber is one of the originals. She's actually like queen of the originals.

I go back down the driveway. I'm shivering. This is the weirdest thing that's ever happened to me. What do I do now? I feel bad about making them go.

Reed looks up at me. 'Does she always copy your work?'

'Sometimes.'

'You shouldn't let her.'

'I don't mind. She's my friend.'

Reed nods philosophically.

Maybe he shouldn't have invited himself and his baby randomly into someone's house, either.

Mercy has finished her bottle of water but she's crying. Reed jiggles her up and down again, trying to get her to stop. It's quite intense when a baby cries. There's a tiny patch of silence when she takes a breath, which makes it even more stressful because you know the noise will start again any second.

'Is something wrong with the baby?' I'm thinking that she really wants her mum, her parents. 'Listen, can you go now?'

'I just need some food and stuff for her, just need to,' Reed scratches a little sore on his hand, 'work out what to do. Need to . . .' his voice trails off and I reckon whatever he's doing, he hasn't thought it through. He looks up at me as if I can save him from whatever trouble he's in, tell him what he needs to do.

But that's ridiculous. Because I never know what to say. And right now, I have absolutely no idea what to do.

Except, 'Okay, I'll boil some water if she's not supposed to have tap water.' Then I see a half-full Pump water bottle on the sink. Mum has a million of them. 'I know, let's give her bottled water. It's really clean. In China that's what you have all the time. No one drinks the tap water there.'

Reed frowns, staring at the water bottle like someone who has to do a prac exam in science and wasn't there for the lessons. 'It's very bad for the environment.'

'I know, but Sadie said babies can't drink water straight from a tap.' And Sadie has little cousins so I reckon she'd know.

Mercy drinks from the bottle again. She seems very thirsty. Reed sits her up a bit on his knee. He has to tilt the bottle so she doesn't drink it all down too fast and then half choke.

Now that the baby is quiet, we can talk.

I start again. 'Can you please tell me what you're doing here.'

'I slept by your heating outlet last night. I had nowhere to go, and it was warm. For Mercy.'

'Okay, but why aren't you at your own house with your own parents? In Ballarat. And what are you doing with a baby? And how do you know my mother's name?'

He answers the second question first.

'I'm her uncle.'

22

'What?'

'I'm Mercy's uncle.' He says it like he is proud to be an uncle. Like he knows it's an important job. This little guy. This little uncle.

'You're pretty young to be an uncle. How old are you?'

'Thirteen. Year Seven. Are you in Year Seven?'

'Year Eight,' I tell him.

He does look too young to be an uncle, but it happens all the time. Winnie at school is an auntie because her dad had a whole family before she was born, then he had Winnie and her sisters. Her oldest sister is thirty something and has two kids.

'You need to answer my other questions and then you need to –'

But he interrupts me.

'I've come to meet my mother.'

Oh. Didn't he have a mother? Like, at home?

'Who's that?'

'Fiona Freeman.'

'What? That's the same name as my mother.'

'I know. I think she's my mother, too.'

'Why didn't you ever tell me? If you knew?'

He sits down. Stands up. Walks in a circle. He might be off his head on something, I don't know. He's sweating, his whole body.

'I was going to,' he says. 'I was always going to.'

3

FORGIVE

I'm about to tell Reed that there must be more than one Fiona Freeman because my mother is not his mother, when I hear the front door slam and the thump of Harry's sports bag on the hallway floor.

Reed looks at me in panic. 'Who's –'

'My brother!'

Reed grabs the bottle and Mercy, picks up the blanket and runs outside into the rain and around the side to the driveway. I close the sliding door.

'Hi!' I call out.

'Hi.' Well, it isn't really hi, it's more a kind of grunt.

Harry goes straight to the fridge.

I've started to sweat even though it's cold. Try to act calm, normal. Should I tell Harry?

'Did you have training? Did you finish early?'

He looks in the fruit bowl. 'Where are the effing bananas? Jesus, I'm supposed to eat three a day.'

I don't answer him. And I'm not going to tell him if he's going to be so rude and awful.

He makes a cheese and Vegemite sandwich and lies on the couch with his headphones on.

I wave to get his attention. 'Mum's having a drink with Troy after work.'

Grunt.

'She texted me.'

Grunt.

'Can you help me make our dinner?'

He takes off the headphones.

'What?'

'Want to help me make dinner?'

'Nup.'

'Harry!'

'I'm binge-resting. It's what we're supposed to do after training.'

'Binge-resting.' I chuck a tea towel at him, trying to get him to smile. 'Lol.'

I sit down on the couch with him like we used to do. These days, he's always at footy training, like three times a week.

'Did you finish early?'

'Some guys went to the gym, but I'm finished, yeah.'

'Oh, right.'

Maybe I will tell him.

'Hey, Harry?'

He picks up his phone. 'Yep?'

'Just before, something stra—'

But he's seen something on his phone and throws it down on the coffee table.

'What was that?'

'Nothing.'

I move to pick up his phone but he grabs my arm. Seriously grabs it. 'It's just the formal.'

Harry got invited by Bella Cheong, a Year Eleven girl at my school. It's all the Year Elevens talk about for like the entire term.

'Oh.' I thought he was looking forward to the formal. 'Which pre's are you and Bella going to?'

'Not going.'

'Not going to the pre's?'

'Not going to the formal.' He glares at his phone. 'Apparently.'

I sit up straight. 'Harry, you can't back out now! Bella will kill you! You can't do that to –'

'I didn't back out,' he says. 'She did.'

'What, she, like, uninvited you?'

'Yep.'

'Why?'

'Didn't give a reason. I didn't really want to go anyway. And now I save the money on the corsage and everything.'

'Oh, right.' I'm confused. The girls in Year Eleven all love Harry. He was one of the first guys to get asked to the formal. And I've never heard of a girl uninviting someone so close to the event.

Harry gets a bowl of like one hundred Weet-Bix and pours honey over them, then milk. He goes back to his binge-resting, puts his headphones on again.

I look through the back windows. Where did Reed go? It's almost dark outside. In summer, the sun doesn't set till about nine o'clock. But now, the night comes in the afternoon. Like it's only half past five.

Maybe I'll never see him again. I'll never know who he was, why he came.

Two parrots with their speedy clockwork wings make a bright green blur through the trees. Even though we live in the suburbs, there are a lot of birds around. From our deck you see parrots, those colourful ones that dart and swoop and have a chirpy call, and the myna birds that are smaller but more aggressive, and the magpies with their warbling song. We used to sometimes see a tawny frogmouth or even a kookaburra, but I haven't seen one of them for a while. There are lots of gum trees but you can hear the traffic hum on the main road not far away. So it's quiet, but not truly quiet. I've lived here my whole life. This was the first house Mum and Dad bought, and then when he left, we stayed.

Fine rain is hanging in the air, making it misty again. There's a little baby out there and it's nearly night. I hope they're getting the V/Line back to Ballarat. I'm sure those trains are heated.

I put the vegetable soup in the microwave, make toast for me and Harry. I'm cross that he never helps, well, he used to help but these days he's such a grump. I want to tell him about this afternoon, because already it feels like something that wasn't real, but Harry would probably tell me I was stupid to let Reed in. He wouldn't even be interested in something unusual like someone appearing in our backyard with a baby looking for our mother. He might not even believe me.

I've tried to talk with Mum about Harry's moods. She says things like it's hard for a teenage boy to be without his dad, and I think it's hard for a teenage girl too, and I don't behave like that.

Mum and I used to talk all the time, but the last couple of months she seems a bit preoccupied. With Troy. But I need to ask Mum if she knows the name Reed Lister as soon as I can. Because he knew her name from somewhere.

It's hard to pin Mum down though because she's so busy. I love my mum but she's always moving. Physios think that moving is the answer to everything. Plus she's got Troy, who seems nice, but when she's not moving, she's out with Troy. I mean, I'm happy for her, I really am. I was starting to feel sorry for her when Harry and I were both going out and we'd leave her smiling bravely, sitting at the kitchen bench with a glass of wine on her own.

But now that Hana's left, I'm the one who's always home. If Mum was here on her own now, I could keep her company. I message Hana. We've got a streak going, since she left in March. Sometimes it's a photo of an interesting word. The last word Hana photographed was written in the sand. BLISS. She used to call me Bliss, like Lissa, Liss, Bliss. I scroll down and read our messages. They've changed. They used to be like we were really talking to each other.

> Want me to send you some of the 234859684 photos I've taken of the reef and the water?

29

We used to message each other like one word and then crack up. We had heaps of in-jokes. But now our jokes have no meaning for her anymore.

I get my notebook, scribble HELP! and a smiley face so Hana knows it's not help I'm literally drowning or anything, but help as in I need your advice! I take a pic and send it.

Harry and I have our soup at the table with our phones. I keep looking past him to the window. 'What are you doing?' he asks.

'Nothing,' I say, 'I'll pull the blinds down, it's freezing in here.' I go over and hold the cold, thin chain for the blind. It's really dark outside now. The glass is so cold it's almost wet. Where's he gone?

I put the bowls in the dishwasher because Harry disappears to his room. Thanks for helping, I say to myself. I wonder where Mum and Troy are having their drink. We've met Troy a couple of times, when he's 'dropped by'. Sadie told me this is how it happens. Her parents read all the books about step-parenting. She told me, 'They'll read this book about how the kids should meet the new partner. Everyone reads it, the same one. First meeting – incidental drop-in, won't stay.'

'He's done that,' I say. The first time, it was Troy popping in to fix the lock on the back door which had broken.

'Second meeting – slightly longer drop-in. Third meeting – dinner at a neutral place.'

'That's what we're up to!'

The third meeting.

When Harry's having a shower, I call Hana but she doesn't pick up, so I message to tell her what's happened. Then I go outside to see if Reed might still be around somewhere. I use the torch on my phone. The dark grass shines, the deck glistens. He must have moved on, or gone home, or whatever. What a strange afternoon. I wonder if I'll ever see him again.

Mum comes home about nine. Harry's in his room and I'm doing homework at the table. She's talking to someone as they come down the hallway. Hang on, is this another incidental drop-in? Was that on the list?

'. . . the girl had fainted . . . sprawled at the tram stop . . . I was heading over . . . schoolkids, men, women, just walked around her. One young girl was trying to help but she didn't know what to do. I mean, what kind of world are we living in?'

Each time I see Troy I get a surprise, because Troy is actually younger than my mother.

The way I found out about Troy was because Sadie's mum saw them at the movies together. At school, Sadie came up to us and said, 'Hey, my mum saw your mum at the movies with a guy who was heaps younger than her!'

'Lol,' said Amber, 'Lissa can't get a boyfriend but her mum can!' I'm not even fourteen yet, I don't actually want a boyfriend, but Amber thought this was hysterical.

I'm not sure that Sadie's book would say this is the best way to find out that your mother has a boyfriend.

'Troy's here because he needs to borrow the camping stove,' says Mum. She unpacks fruit from her shopping bag onto the kitchen bench.

'Hi, Lissa.'

I stand up for no reason. 'Hi, Troy.'

Mum calls to Harry, then goes into his room. I don't know if she'll have any luck getting him to come out and say hello.

I'm standing there with Troy. 'How was your drink, or dinner, or –'

'Good, thanks. Yes, really nice, thanks.'

Troy is good-looking. He's a tradie, he makes furniture. He's suntanned even though it's winter. He's muscly, in his shoulders, across his back, and his calves. More muscly than Harry. Much more than Dad.

Thank god Mum reappears.

'Would you like a cup of tea?'

'Just a quick one, thanks, Fi,' he says. 'As long as I'm not interrupting anything.'

Dad never called mum Fi, always Fiona.

A couple of minutes later, Harry slumps out of his room and plonks himself on the couch. Mum's looking over at him, pleading with her eyes for him to get up and be sociable. He's not going to budge. My brother can be a real arsehole.

'G'day, Harry,' says Troy.

Harry mutters some kind of hello (maybe) from the couch.

Troy looks disappointed that Harry hasn't even got up, so I try extra hard.

'Where are you going camping? Like, with the stove that you need?'

Troy sits at the bench. I stand at the other side.

'Cumberland River,' he says. 'With my brother and his kids.'

I nod. 'That sounds nice.'

'It'll be pretty cold, but the kids love camping.'

I rest my hands on the bench, take them off again, feeling uncomfortable.

'How many kids does your brother have?'

'Three. They're younger than you and Harry. Primary school.'

I want to know if Troy has any kids himself. Mum hasn't mentioned any, but she doesn't talk about Troy much. That must be in the book, too. *Don't go on about the new partner.*

'Anyway, your mum was kind enough to lend me the stove because we thought it would come in handy.'

'Harry, could you go and get it for Troy?' Mum asks. 'You'll need a torch.'

'Haven't got any shoes on.'

'I'll get it!' I say, because I can't stand the tension. Mum hands me the key.

I turn the outside light on, and open the door. Freezing. I go down past the lemon tree to the shed. It's not locked. Harry and I never lock it, but Mum does. I push at the metal door and it slides bumpily away. I shine my phone's torch on the shelf with the camping gear, pull out the little stove. It folds up, it's made of orange metal. There are spider webs on it. We haven't been camping since Dad left.

As I turn around to close the door, I see it. Mercy's bottle, empty in the corner of the shed. And Reed's backpack, too. Where is he? The shed's not that big and he's not here. I head around the side . . .

'Can you find it? Liss?' It's Mum, calling from the back deck.

'Yep, got it,' and I race back up the garden.

Troy's still trying to make conversation with Harry. 'And you're in Year Eleven?'

'Yep,' says Harry, not looking up from the TV that he's turned up loud.

I'm embarrassed by how rude Harry is.

I put the stove down on the bench. 'It's a bit dusty.'

'Looks fine,' says Troy. 'Well, I better get going. Thanks for the tea, and the stove. I'll take good care of it.'

He smiles at Mum. He smiles with his eyes. 'See you later, Lissa, Harry,' he calls.

'See you,' I call back.

Mum follows Troy out to the hallway. I want to look around and see if they might kiss, or if he'd hug her, how they'd say goodbye. But at the same time I don't want to. They're talking softly but I don't hear what they say. I check my phone. No streak from Hana, but Perth is two hours behind so I mightn't see it till the morning.

Troy's cup is on the bench. He didn't finish his tea.

Mum comes back in. She puts the cups in the dishwasher, pushes the door shut. She's stressed out because Harry was so rude.

'I think Troy's a nice guy, Mum,' I say.

'Thanks, Liss.'

She looks over to Harry. 'You could have made an effort.'

Harry stands up. 'You could have made an effort with Dad, and this would never have happened.'

He picks up his phone and heads to his room.

He had that dull look on his face. I always knew things were bad when no matter how hard he seemed to try, he could only ever get his eyes half open. His eyelids sort of hung, sad and hurt and half-mast.

How could I help him?

WEDNESDAY

4

MERCY

Reed and Mercy. They're still here then. Around. Or they were last night. Their names go over and over in my head, all night and then the next morning as soon as my alarm goes off in the dark. Mercy. You think mercy means kindness, like compassion. But I looked it up and it's a bit different from that. Have mercy. It's more like kindness to someone you have power over.

Some names mean something in another language. Fleur. Belle. Some words mean what they mean and also the opposite. Like dust is the stuff that gathers on your mantelpiece, but to dust something is actually to get rid of the dust. And invaluable also means valuable. Dope means good, and also someone who's stupid. A dope. They're called contranyms.

Only one meaning. Mercy.

I have netball training early. Mum's up early too so I can't even go down to the shed and see if his bag is still there. I hope he found somewhere warm to sleep or, better still, went home.

He might have got an early train. I think there's only a few trains to Ballarat each day.

Hana has sent a streak, Phew! It's a seat at the beach and a sign: DO NOT SIT HERE.

I respond,

lol did you?

She must be still asleep because I don't get anything back.

On the way to school, Mum says, like fake casually, 'I thought I might ask Troy for dinner on Friday night.' She looks across at me in the front passenger seat. It's like she's too scared to look at Harry in the back. 'So you can all get to know each other a bit.'

'Isn't he going camping? With his brother and the kids?' I ask.

'That's not until the school holidays.'

Interesting. He didn't need to get the stove yesterday then. Could have been an incidental drop-in number three. I must tell Sadie.

'I've got training till seven,' says Harry, staring out the car window. 'And Dad's coming this weekend. Or have you forgotten that?'

'We're seeing Dad on Saturday,' says Mum in an even voice. 'Can you ask Finn's dad for a lift home after training on Friday?'

Harry shrugs. 'S'pose.'

I don't know why Harry's got all mad about Dad again. It was four years ago, when I was nine and Harry was thirteen. Sure, he's had sad times, we all have, but he seems to be more upset now than he was last year. He might think Troy is going to take Dad's place. Maybe he's jealous that Mum spends time with Troy. He doesn't seem to like another man in the house. In Mum's life.

I don't know why they broke up, really. I think Dad wanted to live overseas and Mum didn't. She's a real homebody. She doesn't like to take risks. He got offered a promotion to set up an office in Beijing. Dad works for a big paint company, making special paints for commercial buildings, aeroplanes, things like that. I don't think either of them were having affairs. Dad and Wendy got married two years ago in Shanghai, where Wendy's family lives. Harry and I went. It was strange being at your own father's wedding. It was like we weren't guests, but some odd thing from a past life, a life he had chosen to leave, to forget. A mistake he had made, maybe. Me in a white dress like half a bridesmaid, and Harry in jeans and a tie like half a man. Now Dad and Wendy are having a baby. Mum, she's never had anyone else that I know of. Except now. Troy. Not like Amber's parents, they have new partners all the time. Harry and I see Dad whenever he comes back here, like he and Wendy will be here this weekend. And we've been to Beijing in the school holidays. We facetime with him every week. Amber says her dad puts money in her bank account, but I don't know if they see each other much.

It's raining again. I'm brushing my hair in the passenger seat and putting it in a ponytail for netball. My hair's long but it's really fine so my ponytails are always thin. I look up each street as Mum drives along. I'm looking out for Reed. I wish I'd got his number, so I could text and see if he's okay, if they're both okay. Who was he? How did he know Mum's name? And Mercy. With that cough.

Sometimes talking in the car is good. I've noticed that Mum often tells us difficult things when we're in the car. All looking straight ahead and not at each other. So I'll try this now, too.

'Mum?'

'Yes?'

'Do you know someone called Reed Lister?'

'No, why?'

'No reason.'

The car slows. Also for no reason.

'Mum,' Harry blurts out, 'you don't have to go forty here, it's a sixty-k zone. You know you can get pulled over for going too slowly.'

'If you can't say anything civil, Harry, can I suggest that you keep quiet?' Mum goes even more slowly. It's a very tense ride to school.

'God, what got her so upset all of a sudden?' says Harry when she's dropped us off outside my school and across the road from his. 'All I said was that she was going slowly.'

He starts to walk off. 'Bye,' I call, 'have a good day.' But he's gone before I finish the sentence.

You can read people, too. 'She's hard to read.' It's a funny expression. I'm often trying to read people. Like Mum, and Harry, just now. But sometimes the language I'm using to read them is different from the language that they speak.

I meet Mia at the lockers and we jog down to the netball courts. 'Here comes the B table,' says Amber as we reach them.

Amber doesn't show mercy.

She's been calling us this since Sadie's party a few weeks ago. It was Sadie's fourteenth birthday, and she had a grazing table and twenty friends over, all girls. Sadie had made place cards for everyone with our names on them. There were two tables – one for Sadie and most of our friends, and one for her younger cousins, her granny and grandpa, parents and people like that. The A table and the B table. Amber and all the others were on the A table. Me, Eliza and Mia were the only friends on the B table.

Then they started calling us that. As in, 'Shh, here comes the B table.'

If we're on our own she calls each of us Little B.

Amber is actually a colour, as well as a name. A honey yellow colour. It's also like a resin, but very hard, you can use it in jewellery. And it's what some people call the yellow traffic light – between Go and Stop is Amber.

Our coach is Grace, who's at uni now but used to go to our school. Grace. Harmony. They're names, but they also mean a feeling or emotion. There was a girl called Harmony at our school. Amber's older sister is a friend of hers. Harmony dropped out of uni and lives in Byron Bay. She's training to be a psychic. When Amber told us, I thought she said that Harmony was training to be a sidekick, and then Amber said, 'No, stupid, that's what you are.'

I am, I'm Sadie's sidekick. I wasn't Hana's sidekick. We were equal. And also I wish I'd said to Amber that I'm not stupid because I get way better marks than her. Like in every subject.

Grace smiles, hands me the Wing Attack bib.

Grace. A name with no hard edges.

I take a picture of the Wing Attack bib and send it to Hana with a bird emoji. Streak done for today.

Training is cold, when we start we're in our trackies and hoodies, but I'm always surprised how, even in really cold weather, if you move you warm up. By the end, half of us are just in our 2XUs and t-shirts.

After training, when we're getting changed, Poppy comes over, sits down on the bench to do up her shoes and says, 'Aren't you embarrassed by your brother? Amber says you should be.'

I'm like, 'What? Is this about the formal? It was Bella who cancelled, not –'

She looks up to the others. 'Omigod, she doesn't even know!'

It's true, I don't know what they're talking about, so I ignore them. They're all on their phones now, anyway. And they've always got some gossipy thing that turns out to be nothing.

I check my phone. Nothing from Hana. These days, sometimes her streak is just a pic of the floor, like just to keep it going. And sometimes it's three days before she gets back to me with any other messages.

As soon as I reach the Year Eight lockers, Amber, Sadie and Krissy run over saying, 'How about the guy with the baby who broke into your house? Were you scared?'

'I just found out now!' says Amber.

'I knew yesterday, I saw them yesterday.' Sadie's breathless with excitement.

'He didn't break in,' I say quickly. 'Sadie, you weren't supposed to tell anyone.'

'She only told us because she cares about you,' says Amber. 'She was worried about you, Lissa.'

I don't think she was worried about me, but what am I going to say? Sadie will do anything to be popular.

'Yeah,' says Sadie, 'I was really worried. Did you call the police?'

'Yeah,' say the others like a chorus, 'what happened?'

Everyone wants to know, but I don't have any of the answers. Where he came from, what he wanted, who he was. It's different, being the centre of attention with the originals. For this one moment, they're interested in me. They gather around, Sadie's all excited that it's her friend who has something to say. They love it when there's something new to talk about – someone's parents get divorced, someone's brother's going out with someone they know, someone has tickets to a concert that other people can't afford to go to. Someone's got called out, someone's got cancelled. Someone's got the new eyeliner they saw on a beauty vlog. A Year Twelve at another school committed suicide. It's all the same to them, just stuff to talk about. Stuff they've seen on Insta. Screenshots from Snapchat, from private Insta stories. Stuff people said about other people. They don't care if it's true or not. It's just stuff.

I wish I could think of something to say. But I say nothing.

'Can't you speak, Little B?' says Amber.

'Of course I can speak,' I say. 'Stop putting me down.'

She laughs. 'I wasn't putting you down, I was sending you up, lol.'

Mum says I need to be more assertive, but even when I try that, Amber has a smarter, meaner thing to say. Then I'm

45

on edge all the time, having to plan how to stop them from being mean. I have a sore neck and shoulders every day after school. Mum says that's stress. And she's a physio, so she knows. I never had to worry about being assertive with Hana. It wasn't a competition.

'Sadie said he kidnapped a baby!' says Krissy.

'He hasn't kidnapped her. He's her uncle.'

'How old is he?' asks Poppy. 'Like a man?'

'No, he's younger than us.'

I don't know what they're going to do with this information, and I feel nervous telling them anything more. 'Look,' I say, 'he's just a kid who's run away. I gave him a sandwich and he's gone now. Story's over.'

But I actually do want to see him again. How did he know my mother's name? And our address? I don't know where he slept last night. It was the coldest night this year, they said on the radio. Ballarat is a long way to get home to. And he has a baby! It's raining again and I'm worried he'll be outside with Mercy.

At lunchtime we sit in the library by the heater on our phones. Poppy and her group is there too and they keep looking over at me. I know they're talking about me. It's cold outside but it feels too hot in the library. Like all the oxygen in the room is used up, so I can't get enough to breathe.

I message Hana. She'll be at school by now.

On the train on the way home from school none of them sits with me. I check my phone. Hana hasn't messaged back. I write a list in Notes. I make lists all the time. Not lists of things to do, but lists of words, thoughts. Sometimes they make me feel better.

Sometimes I think they might become a poem.

Things I love about Hana
Lying in the hammock
Doing the crossword
Her long stripy skirt
Summer
How she laughs with her mouth wide open
The feel of her super-short hair
Her big feet
Her tallness
Her happy voice
Her red glasses
How she's bossy and friendly at the same time
When I'm with her I don't feel worried
She can forgive

A girl from Year Nine gets off the station before me. As she walks past, she says, 'Can't your brother pick on someone his own age? What a dog.'

What was that about?

When I get home, I check the shed. Empty. Reed's stuff isn't there either. Harry's at training like always, so it's just me. I make myself crumpets with honey and check my phone again. Yes! Hana has responded.

Hi wow that sounds weird sorry at school will message later.

It's so good to see her name on my phone. I want to message back immediately but I don't want to be a noodge. That's another of Hana's words – it means to pester or nag someone. Hana says it can be a verb or a noun. To noodge, or a noodge.

I check my Insta. Birthday messages. Parties I don't want to go to but I feel stressed that I'm not invited. 'You need to push yourself more,' Mum says. 'Now that Hana's gone, you need to make some new friends.' But I don't want new friends. I want Hana. You know how some people like a big group of friends and some are happy with one friend, like a best friend? I'm one of those people. Sadie's a bit like that, too, except every term at school the best friend changes.

So I'm scrolling through my phone when I see movement outside, through the glass, on the deck.

He's back. Both of them are back!

'What about Sienna? Where is she?'

'I don't know where she is!' he shouted. 'Sienna's gone, okay?'

5

SERENDIPITY

I open the door. He's shivering, there are half-circle shadows under his eyes. Almost blue. The heavy bedraggled blanket is over his shoulders.

He steps into the back room, holding Mercy partly hidden in the blanket like a small nocturnal animal, the backpack half falling down his arm. His runners are wet, like sodden, they leave little puddles on the wooden floor.

He dumps the backpack. 'Is anyone here?'

'Not till after seven. Hey, where did you go?'

'Can I use your bathroom?'

'It's through there. Do you want me to hold her?'

Mercy's sleeping. Gently, he puts her into my arms, then runs to the hallway. He's so formal. 'Can I use your bathroom?' Lol.

He comes back and answers my question. 'I went to the train station but it wasn't safe, and she was coughing so much I came back and we slept in that shed in your garden. I found some sleeping bags. Hope that's okay? I, um, we had nowhere to go.'

It's kind of bad luck whether it's okay or not because that's what he did. Still, I'm glad they weren't out in the rain.

'Then today,' he continues, 'we went to the shopping centre, where it was warm. We just . . . walked around.'

'I saw your bag, and the bottle, in the shed last night. Lucky Mum and Harry didn't see you.'

His face is dirty, his glasses all smeared. 'I heard someone coming, we went behind the shed. I was going to call to you but your mum came out on the deck.'

Mercy coughs in her sleep.

'Is she okay?'

Reed frowns. 'She might need some medicine. I've been trying to keep her warm. I've run out of her nappies. Eliot only had a few left in the bag. And I think she's hungry again. I'm hungry, too,' he adds.

We make a crumpet with honey for Reed and I have another one as well. I tell him to wash his hands. Then he eats some leftover lasagne from the fridge, and two apples.

'Who's Eliot?' I ask as I dip my finger in the honey and put it in my mouth. 'With the nappies?'

'My brother. Mercy's dad.'

Mercy keeps grizzling, and then when she sees us eating, she starts to cry. It's like she's mad that we're eating and she's not. Her cry makes her cough more. It sounds worse than yesterday. Between cries she's like hiccupping. Her mouth is open wide, her tongue in the middle, her eyes scrunched up with the effort of it all.

I hold her while Reed finishes an apple. She's very wet. 'She really needs a dry nappy,' I tell Reed, I almost shout because it's so noisy with the crying.

'I need to get some. Let's feed her first.'

'Let's boil some water like Sadie said.'

I dip my finger in the jar of honey again. Honey's natural, I'm sure babies can have it. I put my finger in Mercy's mouth. She stops crying – relief! – and sucks on my finger quite hard! It makes me laugh, it almost tickles. Like those rock-pool sea anemones that pull on your finger. Then suddenly she's not interested in the honey and starts crying again.

We have to add some bottled water because Mercy won't stop crying and the boiled water is too hot.

It's hard to work anything out when a baby is crying – all you want to do is stop the noise. I wonder if our neighbours can hear it. We put the warm water in the bottle and Reed feeds it to her. She drinks so fast that she starts coughing again. He tilts the bottle to make her drink slower.

'What are you doing in Melbourne when you live in Ballarat?' I ask him. 'Who do you live with?'

'My parents, and my brother Eliot – until he moved out. He's nineteen now.'

'Okay, you have a mother then.'

'I'm adopted.'

'Oh, right.'

'I only found out on the weekend. I didn't know.'

'Is that why you ran away?'

'Partly.'

'So when you say your mother's name is Fiona Freeman, you mean your – what do they call them?'

'Birth mother.' He's got all the lingo down already.

'Why do you think that's her name? How do you know?'

'I've got an email. That's how I found out I was adopted . . .'

'Your parents didn't tell you?'

'I can show you. Can you pass me my backpack?' He's still feeding Mercy. 'Can you unzip it?' A book, *She'll be Right – Australia's response to climate change*, falls out. Printed articles, I see a picture from 9/11. The burning towers, the crashing planes. We've done it in history, too. He leans over, shoves the book back in and takes out a plastic A4 pocket, like for assignments at school, opens it up and slides a piece of paper across the table to me.

It's an email forwarded by someone called Foster Families Care.

> Dear Mr and Mrs Lister,
>
> I have asked Foster Families to pass this message on to you. Please, if it were at all possible I would like to see the baby. I won't bother you or want contact after this, just to see him once, and see that he's all right would help me a great deal. Please contact me at this email address. fiona_freeman961@yahoo.com
>
> Sincerely,
> Fiona Freeman

'Where did you get this?' The date at the top of the page says 18 February 2006. 'It was written, like,' – I do the math – 'thirteen years ago.'

'I found it on a usb. With some forms that said I was adopted.'

'Are you sure that's what they were?'

He looks at me over the rims of his glasses. 'My parents admitted it, when I showed them what I'd found.'

Wow, what a way to find out that you were adopted. A shock. 'Okay . . . but this email doesn't mean that she's your mother.'

'What else would it mean? And why would they have kept it for all these years?'

'And also it doesn't mean that this Fiona Freeman,' I point to her name, 'is *my* mother. It doesn't make sense. My mother is not your mother.'

'She could be!'

'But I would know! Hang on, you're thirteen, aren't you?'

He nods.

'Are you sure?' He's pretty little.

'I know my own age,' he says, 'I'm not stupid. I'm just small, I was born early.'

Oh, like a premature baby. Ellie at school was premature. She's small, too. But she's smart and everything.

'When's your birthday?'

'January twenty-fifth.'

'Okay, well I turn fourteen next month. July second. That means I'm . . . seven months older than you. So, like, it's kind of impossible.'

Reed pushes his glasses up on his nose. 'Nothing's impossible.'

'Well, some things are.' But I'm not going to go there right now.

'Maybe *you're* adopted too?' he suggests.

'I don't think so.' Anyway, that absolutely makes no sense. Why would Mum adopt a child, then give up the next child for adoption? That couldn't be right. Why am I even thinking this! If my mother had a child and got it adopted then I'd know! I know everything about her life. 'It must be another Fiona Freeman. Also, I asked my mum this morning if she knew anyone called Reed Lister and she said no. Sorry, Reed, my mum's not your Fiona Freeman. I bet there's a few people with that name. It's not that unusual.'

Mercy's fallen asleep. Reed eases the bottle out of her mouth. 'I found three others. I googled them. One's eighty years old, one's twenty-six, and I think one is dead. I found the one who's twenty-six on Facebook and sent a message but I haven't got a reply from her. I found your mum at the Move Australia website, and your home address, here, was listed for private patients.'

I'm thinking I should tell Mum to take our street address off that website.

'I also emailed her work and asked her to contact me, I didn't say why, because she mightn't want people at her work to know. I had to send that one to the Move Australia reception, like the 'info at' email.' He picks up the piece of paper, the old email from some Fiona Freeman thirteen years ago. 'And I emailed her at this address, too. I don't know whether she's got back to me because I had to turn my phone off. Eliot told me to, so that no one would trace me. You know how parents can trace you with that Find My Phone app.'

I nod, looking at the printed email. 'This would be a very old email address. Thirteen years old. Whoever that Fiona

Freeman is, she might have a different email now. I know that's not my mother's email address. Hers is a Gmail.'

'My parents still have the same email address that she sent it to. Still live in the same house, all the same addresses. So she might, too.'

'Do you want to log in on my laptop and see if the Fiona Freeman you sent it to has got back to you? It might have bounced back, if the email is really old. You could also try emailing the Foster Families people, the ones who forwarded it to your parents.'

'I already did that,' he said. 'It bounced straight back.'

I get my laptop and put it on the table. Reed hands me Mercy, who seems to half wake up. I get out the honey. Reed logs in to Gmail. He scrolls down.

Nothing from any Fiona Freeman. Nothing back from the Move Australia address either.

I'm looking over his shoulder, Mercy sucking my finger again. She really likes honey.

'Who's Peter Lister?' I say. There are a heap of messages from him.

'My dad, my parents,' says Reed. He shuts down Gmail and closes my laptop, gently, without reading the messages. Puts his hands on the laptop as if he's blessing it or something. 'Thank you.'

'How many nights have you been gone? They must be worried about you.'

'Two. I found the usb on Sunday and then I wagged school on Monday and went to Eliot's. Then here. With Mercy. So, Monday night and last night.'

'Do you reckon they would have called the police?' My mum would have, definitely. But who knows, maybe Reed runs away every second day.

'Or spoken to Eliot,' says Reed. 'He probably won't tell them he's seen me. I bet he's refusing to speak to them. Sometimes he does that.'

Mercy has woken up properly now, she's coughing and, oh no, starting to cry again. I try jiggling her up and down like Reed does. I try more honey. She arches her back and cries more. I can feel the wet nappy through her clothes.

'Do you reckon she can eat food?' Reed asks.

'I don't know.' How should I know?

'She keeps looking at the banana.'

Then I have an idea. 'What about milk? We've got some milk now.'

I get the milk from the fridge, we heat it up in the microwave and pour it into the bottle. We even put a bit of Milo in it. Warm Milo is good, and Mercy seems to like it. Reed sits down and feeds her. He's smiling because she's not crying anymore. It's such a relief when she stops crying!

When Mercy's drinking her Milo, Reed tells me how he found the usb. 'My parents had been watching this show on Netflix about cleaning up and they were going crazy for it. We were cleaning out the study on Sunday, and there was a usb in the bottom drawer. I actually needed one for my school assignment so I took it, I thought it was an old one of Dad's. There was this folder in it that said ARCHIVE. I opened it and there were some scans of adoption papers, and the email.'

Mercy has almost finished the milk and is starting to squirm. Please don't start crying again. Go to sleep now. Aren't babies supposed to sleep for hours?

Reed walks around, patting Mercy on his shoulder. 'I asked them what it meant and first they said they didn't know, that the usb must be someone else's, but it had ADF on it which is the defence force which is where my dad works so it was his. In the end they said yes, I am adopted.' He stops patting Mercy, as if he's realising a new thought. 'They only told me the truth when they were totally in a corner with no way out.'

'Did you ask them about the email? From that Fiona Freeman?'

'They said they didn't know who she was, they'd never responded to the email she sent.' Mercy's squawking on and off. Reed walks in a circle with her. 'I was so mad. If they weren't going to tell me, I was going to have to find out myself. I looked up the Fiona Freemans, then the next day I took the usb and went to see Eliot. To find out if he knew, like, what he could tell me. If he could help . . .'

'Is Eliot in Ballarat too?'

'No, Coburg.'

'How did you get there?'

'Train. Route follows the Western Highway, stops at Ballan, Bacchus Marsh, Melton, Rockbank, Caroline Springs, Deer Park, Ardeer, Sunshine, Footscray, Southern Cross, then swap lines to Coburg. If I had my phone I could show you on the map.'

It's quite a list, and he says it fast, like he doesn't even have to do that looking up and to the side thing people do when they are recalling something, like a fact, or a place. 'Do you know all the stations off by heart?'

'Yes,' he says quickly. 'And on to the Lilydale line, to your place, here.'

'Do you get trains all the time?'

'No, but I like to know where I am. I've got apps,' he adds. 'The Ship Finder app, the flight tracker app.' He takes a breath. 'Transport apps.'

'How did you find this house without your phone?'

'I made a mental map before I turned it off.'

She's starting up again. A baby's cry is so loud when there are no other sounds. Reed rocks her in his arms, like in pictures of mothers and babies in storybooks. Mercy cries more. She's coughing so much and kind of choking and then . . .

She throws up, all the Milo, all over the floor, and me, and my laptop and Reed, and the email from Fiona Freeman.

'Oh sorry, sorry,' says Reed. 'I'll clean this up.'

Should Mercy even have normal milk? I wipe down my laptop and then google Can babies drink normal milk? Why didn't I google this before the Milo?

'Oh god, they're not supposed to have normal milk till one year of age! It can make them sick. It says NEVER give a baby cow's milk.' Honey also seems to be quite bad. There's all this stuff about something called formula, which now I remember seeing on TV ads. 'You need to get some formula. And nappies,' I tell Reed. I have to yell now because Mercy's screaming, her face red, her arms all stiff, little fists clenched. It's like she's almost forgetting to breathe, she's crying so much.

'How will we get her to stop!' Reed asks me, or himself, or the universe.

None of us knows.

'Let's clean this up and then go to the shops,' I shout over her screaming. 'To the chemist.'

She's, like, soaking wet, with wee and milky vomit.

'Do you have any money?' Reed says between Mercy's screams.

I hand him a Wettex. 'No. Do you?'

'I had to give what I had to Eliot. I can pay you back. I've got money in my bank account.'

'Can't you go to the ATM?'

'No,' he shouts desperately, his glasses moving on his face as he frowns. 'They'll find me. When people go missing the police always check whether they've used an ATM.'

'Should you stay here then? Or hide somewhere, out of sight? And where people won't hear the crying?'

'If I move around with her, she might stop. She did that yesterday.'

Mum has a jar of coins on the bookshelf, and I know Harry has a stash in his room. Should I take money from the jar or from Harry? Mum will notice, and Harry probably won't because he doesn't seem to notice anything at the moment. I go into his room, open the top drawer of his desk . . .

And see that he's written a list too. But it's not like one of mine. This is Harry's list:

Try to talk to her

Call her out

Change schools

Quit footy
Talk to someone else – Who?
Live with Dad?
Kill myself

There's nothing I can do. What rule has been broken? Just stuff that adults talk about, like fairness, respect, truth – stuff that maybe used to happen, but people don't care about that anymore.

The worst thing I could do is defend myself.

6

EARTHFALL

Earthfall, landslide, avalanche, they all mean the same thing.

Suddenly I'm shaking. I don't know what this list means. I don't know what to do with it. I leave it where it is, close the drawer. Leave the room.

Mercy's still screaming. Reed is really agitated. 'Did you get some money?'

'What? No, I'll have to get it from here.' I can't tell Reed what I just saw. I tip the jar upside down. My hands are trembling and I almost drop it. I take about forty dollars in one- and two-dollar coins. Some fall on the floor. I pick them up, shove them in a tote bag from under the sink.

I open the back door. 'Let's go.'

Sometimes when things are totally bad, there's a strange calm that comes over me and all I can see is what to do for this minute, and then the next minute, and then the minute after that. Is that what shock is? The world, my life, feels unreal. I remember this feeling when Dad told us he was leaving. Dad said it's okay to cry, I mean he was even crying, but I just felt as if some part of me had been given one of those injections that makes you numb.

We're out in the street. Mercy's wailing. We walk fast. I lead the way.

Maybe it's not a list? It could be song lyrics or something.

Harry and I used to be really close, even though he's four years older than me. My favourite thing to do when I was little was have a sleepover in his bedroom. On a weekend night, we'd set up a mattress on the floor, we'd talk until late (it was probably only 9 pm), eat chocolate and play UNO and I don't really remember what else we did, only that I loved it. He was so fun, so kind to me. I wanted to be just like him. But since Harry started Year Eleven he doesn't seem interested in anything about me anymore. Or anything about anyone. I don't know what's wrong with him. It makes me feel alone. He must feel alone too. To write that.

As we walk, Mercy seems to have exhausted herself with all that screaming and is falling asleep on Reed's shoulder. She's doing that jerky after-crying breathing that kids do if they've cried for a long time. Poor little Mercy.

'Good girl, Mercy,' Reed is saying. 'We're going to get you some formula, it'll be great.' He looks too young, with his round face and anxious eyes, to be doing this.

It's so quiet now that Mercy's stopped. I can hear Reed's runners as they touch the footpath. I should have got a blanket for Mercy. It's cold out here.

We walk past Hana's street. It's funny but it's actually called Sesame Street. I used to wonder if the street was named before the TV show started. Maybe the word sesame only meant the seeds, back then. This is the corner we used to meet on every morning to walk to the station together. I hate walking past her place now. They have a house-sitter there, it feels wrong that a stranger is inside their home.

We turn right at the roundabout and head up Redstone Road. We're walking at the same pace. I need to make a list, a plan. I need to talk to Harry, but he won't talk to me, I'm sure. I don't know what to do, I feel desperate that I saw that note and now I don't know what to do! I look up at the cold white sky. Then across at Reed, marching along, holding little Mercy against him. What does he think he's even doing, running away with a baby?

'What exactly is your plan?' I ask him. 'Like, you must have got a shock to find out that you're adopted, and you're angry with your parents and all that. But I don't get why you're running away. Or what Mercy's got to do with it. Can't you take her back to Eliot? He's her father, she's his responsibility, not yours.'

He's puffing because we're walking fast and he's carrying a baby, who isn't that heavy but he's been carrying her for like three days now.

'When I found the usb and I knew they'd lied to me I was so angry. I couldn't sleep at all that night. The next day, Monday, I didn't go to school, I caught the train to Melbourne, to Eliot's place. They'd told me not to see Eliot because he's a bad influence on me, but I'd been messaging him and I'd seen him a few times when I was in Melbourne for the school strike for climate change. But they didn't know that. And only I knew about Mercy.'

'Oh, so they don't even know about Mercy? Like, at all?'

He shakes his head. 'They would totally freak.' He winces. 'I actually don't know what they'd do.'

We walk past the hospital. 'Chemist Warehouse is up here on the right,' I tell him. 'Okay, so you went to see Eliot . . .'

'I thought I'd stay with him for a day or two, I wanted out from my parents, and I wanted to find out what Eliot knew about me being adopted, like whether he knew at all. If he knew who Fiona Freeman was.'

'Did he?'

'He'd never heard of her. And Eliot was in a mess. He wasn't actually that interested in what had happened to me, because he needed me to take Mercy. Sienna, that's his partner, had gone to Queensland, like, run off. They were both planning on going, but then Sienna went without him.' Reed pauses. 'And without Mercy.'

We cross the road, jogging to avoid cars. 'Want me to hold her for a bit?'

'It's okay,' says Reed.

'So did Eliot know that you're adopted?'

'He's known for a couple of years. I asked if he's adopted too, but he isn't. I was a bit pissed off with him because he hadn't told me I was adopted when he found out.'

'And he just gave you Mercy? Like, made you take her?'

Reed nods, grimacing like this is all too hard to explain.

'Where did he think you were going to take her?'

'I don't think he really cared. I mean, he cared, but he couldn't really think that through. He wasn't really . . . coping.' Reed looks carefully left and right as we cross a side street, little wrinkles sit along his forehead. 'I mean, it was sort of lucky for Eliot that I turned up when I did . . . Not that he's a bad person, he's just made some bad choices.' Reed speaks wisely, as if he's a counsellor at school. 'I didn't know what else to do. He's my brother. He doesn't have anyone else now. He made me hold Mercy and then he told me to go. He . . . yelled at me. To go. To take her away. From him.'

'Oh, right . . .'

Reed slows down, turns to me as we walk. 'You need to understand that, his place, it's not a good place for a baby. Each time I went since Mercy was born, I got more and more worried. I was keeping a big secret from my parents and I was worried that Eliot and Sienna weren't caring for Mercy like parents should.' I feel a spot of rain, drops darken the footpath in front of us. 'I didn't want anything bad to happen to her,' continues Reed, 'she's only a baby . . . So, like, when he gave me Mercy and told me to go, everything became a bit more . . . complicated.'

I look at Mercy, sleeping. Should babies have dark circles under their eyes? 'Reed, you need to take her back. You can't keep looking after a baby and trying to find someone who sent an email thirteen years ago. And you need to go to school and stuff. They must all be wondering where you are.'

The fine rain looks like mist. We speed up.

'But Eliot can't really look after her. He's got some problems. He'll sort them out, they're only temporary. I bought him a book about addiction, and some nicotine gum so he can stop smoking.'

'Take her to your parents, then. Or maybe to a doctor, Reed.'

'I can't go back home with Mercy,' he tells me. 'Like I said, my parents don't even know that Eliot has a baby. They'd *really* hate Eliot then, even more than they do now. So I'm a bit stuck with Mercy.' He shakes his head as he trudges on, protecting Mercy's face from the rain with his hand like a tiny umbrella. 'I thought that if I could find my birth mother then she might like to, you know, help me out a bit. Maybe even look after Mercy for a while.'

'Why?'

Like, that makes no sense at all.

Like, there is so much that's wrong about that.

'Well, because . . . well, I hadn't really thought about that part.'

'Okay . . .'

'Listen,' Reed cries suddenly, stopping on the street, 'maybe I shouldn't have run away, but I was so mad with them! And I thought Eliot might know who Fiona Freeman is. And then when Eliot gave me Mercy and told me to go, I had *nowhere* to go! I couldn't go home now that I had Mercy, and the only other person I figured might help was my birth mother, Fiona Freeman. She was the only lead I had. I had to fix it, fix this . . . And, and . . .'

It's like he gets to the end of the points on a list and runs out of things to add.

He starts moving again.

From what I know, Reed seems quite smart, like he's carrying around a book about climate change and a folder of articles (that he packed even when he was running away!), and then there's his general knowledge and sense of direction. But he seems a bit unrealistic, too, thinking his birth mother would want to help with Mercy, or even want to know Reed. Or even thinking that he can find his birth mother on his own. Or, like, at all. He looks like a tiny man and he's all serious and sensible, but some of his ideas are like a little kid's, someone who doesn't understand the world very well at all.

I'm probably like that too. I'm a good writer, but I don't get great marks because I don't follow the formula like in Naplan. And I read books about words that are meant for adults, but I can never think of the right words to say when I'm speaking. Maybe Harry, too. He's really smart at maths and actually all subjects at school, and he's great at footy, and he totally looks like a man. But he's not coping with something. What's happening to him that he has to write that list?

We stop at the lights. 'It's good that you were trying to find a solution, but I don't think you have a choice,' I tell Reed.

'I'm trying to do the right thing by my brother.'

'But he can't expect you to look after his baby!'

The rain has stopped. 'Look,' says Reed, 'I know I should go back. But I need to find Fiona Freeman first. I want to know if she's my birth mother. If I go back now, they'll stop me from finding her. They won't help me. They didn't even want me to know I'm adopted. They'll refuse to talk about it. That's what they do.'

The green man lights up, the clicking goes faster. We cross the road.

'They won't want Mercy. They'll give her away, to be adopted. Eliot would never forgive me. They said that they've saved Eliot so many times, and now he's on his own. They can't keep saving him.' Reed marches on, clutching Mercy, head down against the cold breeze.

'So do you have to save him now?' I ask.

No answer from Reed.

'What about Mercy's mother?'

'I told you. She left. And Sienna's quite young,' Reed adds, as if he's, like, thirty-five. 'To be a mother. She's only a bit older than me, than us, I think. She's not that,' he frowns, trying to find the right word, 'reliable.'

I look at little Mercy, her head resting against Reed's shoulder.

God, what are we going to do?

'Okay,' I say, 'we'll get the formula, and the nappies, and then, I'm sorry, Reed. You need to go home. My mother doesn't know you. You can't keep hiding in our shed. We can tell my mum if you like, but she'll only send you home. Or she'll call the police. And your parents mightn't like it that Eliot has a baby, but they won't just throw Mercy out into the street.'

The hoodie has fallen over his face, he pushes it back with his free hand. We cross the railway line, we pass Coles. 'Do we go in here?' he asks me.

'No, Chemist Warehouse will be cheaper.'

We're nearly there. I see the sign with the red house and the big loud letters.

'Okay,' says Reed, 'but please, can I make sure Fiona Freeman isn't my birth mother first. If she's not the right one, then I'll go. I just . . . I need to give myself every chance.'

'But Reed, I've asked her! She doesn't know you. She's not the right one.'

'She might not know my name. Can you ask her if she had any other children? Can we ask one more time?'

'How could she have had both of us? We've already talked about this, it makes no sense.'

'What about your dad? Would he know? Could you ask him?'

'Maybe, but they're divorced and he lives in Beijing. I can't facetime him and say, by the way did Mum have another child?' I could ask my aunty, Dad's sister Jo, but she's quite OTT, I don't want to talk to her about it. 'Dad will be here this weekend though. I can try to ask him then if you like.' We pass the nail place, the café. 'God, why didn't your parents tell you? I thought kids got told if they're adopted these days?'

'I don't know.'

Mercy's waking up again. Don't babies ever sleep for more than like twenty minutes?

'People will be looking for you,' I tell him. 'You should have stayed hidden, back at my place, I could have come on my own.'

'They'll think I'm in Ballarat.' He pauses. 'Or they might have looked at Eliot's place. But Coburg's a long way from here. I've only been gone two nights.'

Two nights is a long time to be a missing person. 'Should we make a list? Of what you can do?' But even as I say this, I wonder how any list is going to help him. And I have also reminded myself of Harry's list. The last item is sitting in my head in portrait mode. I need to tell someone. But who?

Just as we get to Chemist Warehouse, Mercy starts again. People are staring at us. 'That baby's too noisy,' says a little kid walking past with his mum, his hands over his ears. His mum slows down, looks at us. I think she's about to say something, but then she walks on, taking her little boy's hand from his ear so she can hold it.

'I'll stay out here,' says Reed, pacing up and down. Mercy is breathless with her coughing and crying. Her little body is shaking and stiff at the same time. 'Can you get the stuff?'

Chemist Warehouse is really confusing, with long narrow aisles and signs in front of bottles of pills and powders, and they also sell chocolates and mineral water, make-up and health food. It feels crowded, even though there's not a heap of people in there.

I grab a blue plastic shopping basket. There's a whole aisle of nappies. They're expensive. They only come in big packs. Like $34.99. I can't reach half of them because the shelves are so tall. I see a special on thirty nappies for $16.99. The formula comes in tins, boxes and plastic packets. For all different age babies. I look for three to six months. I can hear Mercy screaming outside. Organic, original, lactose intolerant, they're all like twenty-five dollars each. Should I get her a dummy as well? That might stop her crying. There's a dummy on special for six dollars. I put it in the basket. Baby wipes, oils and powders, different creams, do babies need all this stuff? What does Mercy need? I get two sample packs of formula, like in a sachet, because they're only eight dollars. Should I get a baby yoghurt thing, the kind sportspeople have except for babies? It's all so expensive, I don't know if I'll have enough money. I grab a onesie from the sale rack because Mercy's is so filthy and every time I look at it, it makes me feel tense.

In the end I have three dollars left. I buy two Lindt balls at the counter.

A baby that won't stop crying makes everyone anxious. When I get outside, even people walking past us are grimacing.

'I couldn't get much formula because you need the nappies as well.'

'Hey, Lissa!'

Amber and her mother are coming towards us.

'Walk away,' I mutter under my breath to Reed. 'I know them. Walk away!'

He can't hear me over Mercy's screaming. I push him a bit. 'Go away.' He doesn't understand.

'Hi.' They've reached us. I stand there, next to Reed and a screaming Mercy.

'Hi.'

Amber's mother turns to Reed and smiles. 'And what's your name?' she says over Mercy's crying.

He's holding Mercy on his hip with one hand and offers his other hand to shake hers. He is so formal and polite! 'Re—'

'This is Ryan! My cousin Ryan. And Mary,' I add, 'another cousin.'

'Looks like your cousin has his hands full there.'

Amber says something to her mum. It's hard to hear, but I think she says, 'It's not her cousin.'

Mercy's getting louder and more furious.

'That baby's cold,' says Amber's mother. 'She should have more clothes on.'

Amber knows Reed must be the guy Sadie was talking about. She nods to her mother with a smug little smile.

'Are you, um, shopping?' I ask them, because I don't know what else to say.

'Yeah, shampoo and things.'

'Right. Anyway, we better get going. Gotta feed Mary and . . . things.'

'That baby doesn't look well,' says Amber's mum.

'She's hungry. Come on, Re . . . Ryan, let's go.'

We walk away, back towards the railway line and home. I get out the dummy and try putting it in Mercy's mouth but she spits it out and it falls on the footpath.

'That was good you didn't say our names.'

'Yeah, I don't know how I thought of that so quickly. Not like the wit of the staircase, which is normally what I have.'

'What's that?'

'Doesn't matter, I'll tell you some other time.' It's too hard to talk when Mercy's crying.

'Who were they?' Reed asks.

'Amber, from school, and her mother, Lorraine, like, the biggest gossip.'

Reed's eyes widen.

I nod. 'She'll tell everyone she knows.'

I read that if you're my age and you like another guy, it could just be a stage.

I read that like thirty times.

A stage.

I could wait for it to go away.

7

JOY

Such a sweet, short word. It means only joy.

We get home and Reed changes Mercy's nappy. He's better at changing a nappy than I would be – I wonder if he's YouTubed it – but she still cries. I turn the heater up, it's only just after five-thirty but it's dark already. Then I mix up the formula. It's hard to focus on the instructions on the packet because Mercy's crying even more, and she keeps crying until the bottle is ready and Reed feeds her and she drinks it all in like three minutes, which makes me think of those baby calves you feed at the animal nurseries that come to fetes.

Then she falls asleep in his arms. Phew! It's like doing meditation in the hall at school when everything finally becomes quiet and calm. At last!

We sit on the couch and eat the Lindt balls. Reed holds Mercy against him. Her little hand is resting on his shoulder.

'How long before your brother gets home, or your mum?'

'Not till about seven-thirty.'

'Are you sure? Any friends coming over?'

I shake my head.

I feel so relieved that she's stopped crying. 'Do you want to put her down somewhere?' I say. 'Like we could make a bed for her?' Reed's been holding her for hours. She's not that heavy but your arms can go a bit numb.

We arrange the cushions on the couch so that she won't roll off, and make a little nest for her. Reed lowers her gently into it. I get a blanket from the hall cupboard. The blanket's way too big so we drape it over the cushions. It's one that my aunty Jo knitted for us – bright, random stripes and squares. Dad always hated the rugs she made, he'd put them away in a cupboard, then we'd have to get them out when Jo came over and pretend they'd been on the couch the whole time.

Mercy looks peaceful for the first time since I've met her. I have a feeling – is it a memory? – of being warm and enclosed like this.

We sit down. Reed rests his elbows on the table, chin in his hands.

'Have you had any sleep?' I ask him.

'Not really. Is she in your year at school, that girl outside the shop?'

'Amber, yeah. I'm in her friendship group, but I wouldn't really call her my friend.'

'What about the other one who copies your homework, is she a friend?'

'Sadie? Yep, she's a friend.' I suppose.

Reed nods, yawns.

'My best friend's Hana, but she's moved back to WA.'
I remember that she hasn't responded to my message. Or sent
a streak today. I check my phone. Still nothing.

We sit there in silence. We both know that sooner or later
we're going to get around to the topic of Reed going home.
I feel tired now, too. Exhausted. I look towards Harry's room.

'I've got three best friends,' says Reed.

'Oh, right.' I can't really concentrate.

'Ali and Olin are in my year at school, and Tess goes to a
different school now, but we all live near each other.'

'In Ballarat.'

'Yeah. We're in the School Students Climate Change Action
Group. We go to the rallies, you know the school strike for
climate change?'

I nod. 'I went with Hana. Her mum and dad went too. My
mum and dad, they're not really into politics.'

'Mine aren't either,' says Reed, taking off his glasses. 'They
hate it that I'm involved. They think it makes me anxious.' He
frowns, cleaning his glasses with a blue-and-white check hanky.
I mean, who carries a hanky in their pocket unless they're like
ninety years old? Then he looks up, half laughs. 'Except, yeah,
they aren't actually my parents.' Reed shakes his head. 'Now I
have to rethink everything. I'm even thinking about my glasses.
No one in my family wears them. I needed them from when I
was like six years old.'

'That doesn't mean anything, really,' I tell him. 'I wear
glasses too, for reading the whiteboard at school, and no one
else in my family does. Some people just have better eyesight
than others.'

It's quiet, except for Mercy's snuffly breathing. I think of Ballarat, of Reed's parents up there. It's a gold rush town, we went there on an excursion in primary school. The site of the Eureka Stockade and all that. That's actually all I know about Ballarat. What would they be doing? Like, would you still go to work if your child had run away?

Outside, it starts to rain – that steady, straight rain with an even rhythm. Reed carefully puts his glasses back on.

'I'm glad we weren't caught in that,' I say. 'Look how fast it's falling.'

He stares out the window. 'Yeah, it's heavy.'

I check my watch. An hour and a half before Harry and Mum are due home.

Reed turns to me. 'Have you ever seen it when rain turns to snow?'

'No, I don't think so.'

'Sometimes it happens in Ballarat. It's like everything slows down,' he pauses, looks over at little sleeping Mercy, 'becomes soft. Quiet.'

We sit there for a while longer. Then I put the wet nappy in a plastic bag and go outside to the bin, shove it under other bags of rubbish. I come back inside, out of the rain. 'I'll ask Mum again tonight if she knows anything at all about you, or anything about any baby thirteen years ago. But tomorrow, you have to go back to your own family.'

We watch Mercy, sleeping on her back. 'I promised Eliot I'd look after her,' Reed says quietly. She's making a little snoring noise. 'My parents will be . . .' he pauses, like he doesn't want to say the word, 'devastated. My mother might have a nervous breakdown or something.'

'*You* might have a nervous breakdown if you have to keep on hiding her! That's not very fair of Eliot,' I have to add, 'putting you in this position.'

Reed just stares at Mercy in her cosy nest, as if he can't bring himself to admit that Eliot has made things this difficult for him.

'How long ago did he move out?' I ask.

'About two years ago. He was seventeen. They didn't chuck him out, but they didn't stop him going, either. He was pretty bad, but they should have made him stay. They didn't want me to end up like him. That made me feel guilty – like I was the reason they didn't stop him, because they wanted his bad influence out of my life.' Reed traces lines on the kitchen table with his finger, tiny grooves in the timber. 'No parent should ever get rid of their kid.' He looks up. 'And they told him not to contact me.' Reed rubs his eye, dislodging his glasses for a second. 'You can't ban someone from seeing their brother. Anyway, I'm not like him. They don't need to worry about that. We're totally different.'

'Harry and I are pretty different, too,' I say.

'He won't be home till after seven, that's right, isn't it?' asks Reed.

'Yep.'

'It's so warm in here. Nice for Mercy.'

I nod.

'Like, Eliot got his Ls the day he turned sixteen. I won't do that.'

'I don't reckon I would either. But Harry loves driving.'

'I'm scared of driving at night,' says Reed. He puts his glasses neatly on the table, rubs his eyes again. 'I'm actually scared of driving. When you think about it, basically you're in control of this steel box moving around, and random strangers are in other steel boxes. Like, you're trusting that everyone on the road is a reasonable person who will do the right thing.'

I'd never thought about it like that, but he's right. 'My mum hates driving under bridges,' I say. 'It's like she holds her breath each time she goes under one.'

Reed nods. 'And what's to stop a driver at the lights from just going through? Deliberately, or by being distracted? And going fast, I mean you could accidentally hit someone or something. Or a truck could come past and not even see you. Truck drivers fall asleep sometimes, they have to drive all night, and think about how heavy a truck is.' Reed pauses. 'Eliot lost his Learner's like a month after he got it. Driving without a supervisor.'

'Right . . .'

'He had a friend in the car, but he was only on his Learner's too. Hopefully Eliot's learnt his lesson. I think he would have.' Reed nods, his eyes wide, trying to convince himself of what he's saying. 'I think he'll be more responsible when he gets his proper licence.'

Mercy coughs, half wakes herself up again. The poor thing, that cough must be waking her up whenever she gets to sleep. But she's not screaming, which is an improvement. Maybe the formula made her feel better. She's making cute little noises like a baby animal. Squeaks.

'Do you think we could give her a bath? And change her into the new thing you bought her?' Reed asks. 'Like, if no one will be home for a while? She's pretty dirty. I am, too, but it's worse if you're a baby.'

'Oh, okay.' I remember how warm water always helps calm me, hopefully it's calming for babies as well.

'If I have to go home, I want them to see that I looked after her properly. Eliot, too.'

I'm relieved that he's thinking about going home. It's what he needs to do.

'I'll go and put the bath on. And Google said you can give a baby mashed banana so want to try that?'

I mash up the banana and Mercy seems to like it. We try to feed it to her with a teaspoon; it takes her a long time to eat like one quarter of a banana and bits of it keep coming out of her mouth and we have to push it back in with our fingers. Reed and I eat the rest of it. We also get it on our clothes, the table, the floor and the kitchen bench.

I don't know how to bath a baby, and neither does Reed. I make it warm, not too hot. Reed undresses her. She has a rash that looks pretty bad, red with even redder spots where the lines of her nappy were, on her tummy and her chest, and a bit on her arms, too. But she doesn't seem to mind when we put her in the water. Reed pulls up his sleeves and cradles Mercy in his arms. He's got smooth olive skin, no freckles.

'Should we use proper soap?' he asks.

I think of the long aisles of Chemist Warehouse. All those things that babies must need that we don't have. 'Maybe just a bit?'

Reed washes Mercy's little body. She kicks her legs but she doesn't cry.

'I wonder what that rash is?'

'Yeah, it's spreading down her arms.'

'And it's on her neck and behind her ears, see?' I'm a bit worried, a rash is never good.

But then our worries leave us because Mercy looks up at Reed, really looks at him like she might be trying to tell him something, then she smiles at him, and then she smiles at me.

When Mercy smiles, her mouth is wide open. Her eyes crinkle up a bit, and her whole face moves with the smile. A feeling fills up inside me.

I think it's joy.

Reed and I smile back at her, then we smile at each other, and it's like something collapses inside me and I might cry.

'Do we wash on her head? With a bit of soap?' he asks me. 'Or should we use shampoo?'

'She doesn't have much hair, maybe just the soap then.'

We don't want the soap to get in her eyes. Mercy blinks the water away. Her tiny eyelashes all go together. Pale blue eyes. I think she likes being in the bath.

'Should we put something on the rash?' Reed asks.

'Reed, I don't know! I don't know any more than you do.'

'Oh, cool, sorry.'

We get her out and wrap her in my towel. The bathroom floor is really cold, so we take her into my room and lie her on my bed in the towel. I turn on the light – Jo gave it to me, it's one of those big round paper ones, a pale orange colour. It gives my room a soft warm glow.

'You've got a lot of books,' says Reed when he sees my Ikea bookcase against the wall.

'Yeah, I still like reading books.' I pat Mercy dry with the towel. 'History. Biographies, I like. And some are like my notebooks and stuff.'

Mercy kicks her little legs as I dry them. I can feel her tiny bones. It makes me worried. Babies on YouTube have those little fat rolls and a round tummy. We put on a new nappy from the Huggies pack. And the new onesie, it's blue with orange kites on it. It has a lot of press studs. Together we get them all matched up. I feel so much happier because Mercy looks better. More like other babies. She feels cold now though, so I get my polar fleece top and we wrap it all around her. I wish I'd had enough money to buy one of those sleeping bags that babies have.

We're just coming out of my bedroom with Mercy all clean and warm when I hear the front door open. A bag hits the floor in the hallway. Harry.

I close my bedroom door. Mercy starts to whimper.

'I thought you said –'

'He has footy training! Till seven!' I whisper. I check my phone. Twenty-five past six. What's he doing home?

'Sshh, Mercy,' I say. 'Please.'

I can hear Harry in the kitchen.

Reed is afraid to move. So am I. Mercy coughs. She whimpers again.

I hold my breath. She's going to start.

I grab my phone and tap Spotify, turn up the volume. It's on shuffle and I've never been so relieved to hear 'Shake it Off' in my life. Even Mercy gets a shock and doesn't cry, she just looks startled. I bounce her up and down to Taylor Swift. I'm actually dancing around with Mercy. She smiles again, so I half sing the song to her. She really likes music! Reed's sitting on my bed, watching us. Wow, imagine if I'd known that the first time I'd have a boy in my room it would be like this. If it wasn't so incredibly stressful it might be fun.

Harry used to always come in and say hi when he got home but he never does that now and tonight I'm glad.

When we're sure she won't start crying, I turn down the volume a bit and we listen out for Harry. His bedroom door closes and I hear his computer start up.

I open the door. We look out. The coast is clear. 'Quick,' I whisper, 'go down to the shed! I'll come when I can.' Reed escapes with Mercy, all wrapped up in my polar fleece.

After a few minutes, I go and knock on Harry's door.

I open it. He's sitting at his desk, staring at his phone.

'Hey.'

Grunt.

'You're home early. From training.'

Silence.

'Harry –'

He turns around, angry. 'What!'

'Jesus, don't worry about it.' I walk out. He's impossible.

'Close the door,' he shouts at me.

I stand in the hallway, stare at the photos on the wall of me and Harry smiling, arms around each other on the Great Wall near Beijing. I want to tell him about Reed, I need him to help me! I want to ask him about the list. I come back to his doorway. The drawer of his desk is closed. Maybe the list is old? He could have written it ages ago.

'Harry, is everything okay? Harry?'

He swivels around in his chair to face me.

I think he might be about to tell me something . . .

'I've got a test tomorrow, I have to study.'

'Can we just –'

'I said I have to study.'

He's so cold, so angry, it's like the time when we could talk to each other is ancient history. I can't even imagine it anymore.

I close his stupid door.

I finish wiping up the bits of banana. Mum should be home soon, so I get some food for Reed. There's only one banana left so I can't take that. I make two peanut butter sandwiches, grab a couple of apples, and in the pantry I find some protein bars, a bag of almonds and half a block of cooking chocolate. I fill a hot-water bottle. It's so wet and dark outside. I make up another bottle for Mercy, and get the nappies from my bedroom.

He's sitting down in the shed with her. He's found Harry's sleeping bag, and I get them the big one that Mum and Dad used to share when we went camping. It's still totally freezing. Too cold for a baby. Reed leans against the shed wall, he's shivering and Mercy seems to be as well. He's got a torch, I've made it as comfy as I can for him, but this isn't like making a cubby when you're a kid.

'Tomorrow you go,' I tell him.

He looks up at me, nursing Mercy, sad. 'Just ask your mum tonight, please?'

'Turn the torch off, or point it that way. I don't want Mum or Harry to see light down here.' Suddenly I feel angry with him, what am I supposed to do?

As I run back up to the house and out of the cold, I think that maybe he just won't go. He's friendly, he's kind and gentle, but he also seems quite stubborn. I can't make him go. If I dragged him off the property he could simply walk back in, carrying Mercy on his hip like a small mother.

This can't last.

When you're a little kid, you can make mistakes like taking something that wasn't yours, or saying something mean, or lying to your parents about how many biscuits you'd eaten. But those things won't change your life.

Then when you're older, you can make a mistake that you can't come back from.

THURSDAY

8

SPLASHDOWN

Harry says he doesn't have a favourite word, but I know he used to like the word splashdown. It's the landing of a returning spacecraft on the sea. Sometimes a parachute is launched on the way down, to soften the landing into the water. Splashdown.

I don't even know where he heard it.

I realise when I wake up the next morning and there's nothing from Hana. We've lost our streak.

I lie back in bed, pull my doona up to my chin. My body's warm but my face is cold. My ears. I breathe slowly. I stare at the wall, at the map of the world that Dad gave me when he moved to Beijing. And all the little origami animals I made with Hana on my shelf. Like a million years ago. I don't want to get up.

I message her.

> You broke our streak! Doesn't matter we can still text like we always do.

Do we? Still? I don't want to sound too disappointed, too needy.

I don't get a chance to ask Mum anything more about babies from thirteen years ago, because last night I was already asleep when she got home and this morning we're all rushing to get ready and I have to leave early for netball.

Amber's not at school. This isn't unusual because she gets migraines. I tell the others that Reed has gone now. It's not the exact truth but I've told him he has to go, so it's kind of the truth. Like, he's going today.

When I get home from school, I look in the shed but they're not there. Reed's stuff is there, so he can't be far away. I feel stressed, knowing he's near but not knowing where. In my head I try to pretend that he's gone back home, but I know he hasn't, so it doesn't really work.

Mum's out again. She said it's a meeting, told us we could get Uber Eats, which is what she does when she feels guilty. Harry orders the food. We get pizza, which is what he wants. I wanted pho but I can't be bothered arguing with him, and it costs more to get stuff from two places.

We eat at the table with our phones. My neck hurts, my shoulders.

'How was your test?' I ask him.

He shrugs. 'Okay, I think.'

It would be nice if he asked me how my day was. He eats more pizza and looks at his phone.

'Harry, I –'

His phone buzzes. He stands up, says hi, goes into his room

and shuts the door. I'm about to get up to listen when he comes out again.

'Who was that?' I ask.

He doesn't look at me. Sits down, takes another slice of pizza. 'No one you know.'

We eat in silence. I reckon the phone call was something to do with whatever that rumour is.

'Has Mum texted you?' I ask.

'Nuh.' More pizza.

'Jesus, Harry, can you leave some for me?'

Before Mum met Troy she would never have stayed out like this. Where is she? She was out last night and now tonight as well. If it was only an after-work meeting, she'd be home by now. Has she gone back to his place? Where does he even live? What are they doing there? I suppose it's okay that she's out late, because Harry and I are both teenagers, but sometimes I go and kneel on the couch in the front room like a little kid, watching out the bay window for the headlights of her old blue Golf coming up the street to our driveway.

I want to go down to the shed. Harry's watching the footy. A Thursday night game. I pick up the empty milk carton.

'Just going to put this in the recycling.'

Harry ignores me.

I tap the torch on my phone and run down to the shed, open the rough sliding door. 'Reed?'

They're sleeping. Both of them under the sleeping bags. Mercy is snoring and wheezing. She's a very loud-breathing baby, or maybe all babies breathe like that. I look at them and I can't think of the right word because I don't even know what

I feel. Her head is on his chest. I can't make a list for what to do next, I have no idea what is going to happen with Reed and Mercy.

Another night. Four nights now. His parents must be going crazy.

I come back inside. The footy's over. Harry turns off the TV. 'Who won?' I ask, because we've hardly spoken to each other all evening, and I suppose I'm still trying.

'Hawks.'

'Was it a good game?'

'It was okay.'

'Mum's pretty late.' It's ten-thirty.

Harry doesn't respond. He's going to his room. Is this what our life is going to be like now? Mum never home and Harry never speaking?

'Hey, apparently Amber's saying I should be embarrassed by you. What an idiot.' I roll my eyes, trying to make it a kind of light-hearted joke that we can share. 'She so has the biggest crush on you.'

He turns around quickly to face me. 'When? When did she say that?'

'I don't know, yesterday, the day before, it's no big deal.'

'Did she say why?'

'No . . . Harry, I think it was a joke.'

'Then don't tell me about it!'

'No need to bite my head off.'

He's storming off down the hallway. I call after him, 'Harry, is everything okay? You can tell me if something's wrong. You can trust me.'

'I can't trust anyone,' he shouts, not looking back.

I go to my room, check my phone, turn off my light, try to sleep. I think of Reed and Mercy in the shed. Mum, wherever she is. I message Hana.

Have I done something wrong?

I still can't sleep. Where the hell is Mum?

Whenever I can't sleep I make lists in my bullet journal.

Things I don't know
How to help Harry
What to do about Reed
What Mercy needs
How not to lose Hana
How to get Mum to talk to me
How to ever make any new friends
How to make things okay again

I lie there for like two hours. I'm often asking myself the question, Will things be okay? When Mum and Dad separated, when Hana left, when Harry started to move away from me, when Amber ramped up her meanness. But what does okay even mean? Like, the word? The dictionary says it means 'satisfactory but not especially good', but it feels more reassuring than that. Like when you say, 'It's okay', you're saying that things will work out – maybe not perfectly, but they will work out.

But will they?
How will they?

We insult each other all the time.

Is that some kind of caring?

Is that what guys are supposed to do?

What should I do?

I save the photo.

FRIDAY

9

MOVE

The next morning I don't see Mum at all because she has an early class on Fridays and always leaves before seven. There's a sticky note on the bench. *Sorry I was so late last night. Meeting went on for ever. Will be home early tonight. Remember Troy coming for dinner. xxxmum*

Harry's in the kitchen, so I can't go down to the shed, he'll see me through the back window.

There's a message from Hana.

> Bliss! course not. Really busy. We go to the beach after school. Come and stay next holidays!

Seeing that makes me feel better. It's amazing how some small words on a screen can totally transform your mood. And I don't just miss Hana, I miss her whole family. I used to love going over to her place, hanging out with her little brothers, her mum and dad. Their house was always busy, and loud in a happy kind of way.

I take a pack of two-minute noodles from the pantry, grab an orange and train to school with Sadie. She asks about Reed. 'Amber told me she saw you with him. Her mum's going to tell your mum.' She smiles. 'You told them he was your cousin.'

Words disappear inside me.

'He's going home today, back to Ballarat,' I try to sound casual as we walk into school, 'so there's no need for Amber's mother to do that.'

We get to the lockers and Amber's talking about it already. 'We might even go to . . . Shh, here she is!'

'Amber, please, it's got nothing to do with you.'

'I'm just worried. I mean, we're only trying to protect you. And anyway, you know it's a crime, if that guy's taken the baby then you're harbouring a criminal.'

'Two criminals,' says Poppy.

Amber's eyes narrow. 'Might be.'

'What did they mean just now, about two criminals?' I ask Sadie as we're walking under the breezeway to assembly. 'He's not a criminal, and Mercy, she's a baby.'

'No, it's the stuff about your brother.'

'What stuff?'

'Just rumours, I think.'

I thought of Harry's list. 'My brother seems pretty down at the moment. Do you know something about it?'

'Not really,' says Sadie. 'There's some stuff on people's private stories . . .'

'Amber's private stories? On Insta?'

'Like, no offence, but Amber says he uses girls.'

'What?'

'She reckons she's got screenshots to prove it.'

'He doesn't even go out with girls. And what would Amber know about my brother anyway?'

'Just my personal opinion, but he could have used her.' Sadie shrugs, giving her 'whatever' look. But she's got this little tic in her eyelid, like a fluttering under the skin. 'Bell's gone, we better hurry!'

Sitting in maths, I can't concentrate at all. I look across at Sadie. She has to sit by herself because she's 'easily distracted'. That's another subject where she sometimes takes photos of my work.

Sadie is pretty – without trying. Her hair is the colour of honey, she has no freckles, sparkly blue eyes. How can people get both the olive skin and the blonde hair? And her teeth! She's like the only girl in Year Eight who hasn't had to get braces. She's like a picture you'd see on Insta and the caption would be 'pretty girl'. Mum says her looks are 'generic'. That means not specific. That there's no detail to Sadie. Just, 'pretty'.

But that tic is specific about Sadie. So I'm thinking she's not that generic.

At recess, I ask Sadie about those rumours again and she says, 'Okay, don't tell the others that I've shown you this. I'm only showing you because I'm your friend.'

'Show me what?'

We go down behind the art room. She holds her phone out to me. 'You would have seen it anyway,' she says.

It's Instagram. Black and white. It's a nude, but it's only the top half, someone's boobs. It's cut off at the neck. There's a thinking emoji over each nipple. Okay, that's pretty bad, someone's posted a nude that was probably sent privately. I've never sent a nude, but people do.

'Who posted this?'

Then I see the name of the account.

@rateyear8_BGS

'Who's that?' I ask.

'Some guys who are rating Year Eight girls, we think.'

There are a heap of comments. Some trying to guess who it is, a lot giving a score out of ten or asking to see more in the next post. And a few saying what a low act it is to post this. Comments about the photo itself, the size of her boobs, guessing the colour and shape of her nipples. Makes me feel sick.

'This is gross, what's my brother got to do with it?'

Sadie hands me her phone. 'Read down the comments.'

But I'm looking more closely at the pic. It's a bit blurred, but you can see the girl's long dark hair and her chin, her shoulders. A dark, oval-shaped freckle just above her collarbone.

'Is that Amber?'

Sadie nods excitedly. 'Someone's already outed her, this morning. Look!'

There's a comment from Amy someone.

Amber Pembrose?

Oh god, poor Amber.

'He didn't even disguise that. No offence, but your brother's a creep. Amber's so upset. She pleaded with him to take it down.'

'What? Harry?'

Sadie grabs the phone, scrolls down further, finds a comment, points to it. It's from Amber.

@harry_freeman002 please take this down.

'What?'

Sadie looks almost pleased. 'Amber told us he made her send him a nude. We reckon he made this whole Rate Year Eight profile. It's him, Lissa.'

That really annoys me about Sadie. She's so sure that she's right about everything.

'When did this even go up?' I take the phone again and look at the times.

'Last night,' says Sadie, 'like, late last night. It's private, request to follow if you like.'

'As if I want to follow this,' I say quietly.

'You know he made out with her,' Sadie continues, 'and then he didn't call her. Look at her post, her private Insta story. Hang on, you're not in her private group. She made a live video, did you see that? Wait, I'll show you the comments in her private group.'

How can people write this stuff? About their age difference, what a creep Harry is, even that he has an STD and all this crap. It's so awful but it's also completely ridiculous.

It's like for a minute Sadie forgets she's talking to me, Harry's actual sister, and she's just enjoying the gossip with another friend. 'And omigod he's in Year Eleven and she's Year Eight!' She looks down at her phone. 'Oh look, Amber's commented again!'

She moves closer to me. 'I mean, it's just my personal opinion, but this is really bad, Lissa. Amber's going to report it to Instagram.'

I hand her back her stupid phone. 'He never made out with her!'

'He wouldn't tell you if he did.'

'He tells me everything.' Or he used to, I suddenly think. But I can't believe he'd ask Amber for a pic or that he'd share something like that with other guys.

'Can I have a look again?' I ask. 'My phone's in my locker.'

I'm scrolling down the comments, more coming in all the time. There are a few from names I recognise, guys who play footy with Harry. Some just the laughing emoji, some bagging Harry, and some rating Amber and thinking it's all a great joke. And lots of people tagging other people.

'If he made this post, then why isn't he deleting half of these comments? That are totally trashing him?' Nothing about this makes sense.

'He's probably in class, or his phone's in his bag.'

'When is he supposed to have made out with her?' I ask.

'See.' Sadie smiles. 'You don't know everything about him. It was after a footy game,' she says, kind of breezily. 'At a party for their coach in the clubrooms afterwards? Amber's brother plays in the same team, remember. Her whole family was there.'

'He wouldn't have done that. He's not even interested in girls.' It's the first time I've said that out loud.

Sadie shakes her head knowingly. 'A lot of girls are saying

that it's typical of him. Even girls at other schools. Guys, too. It's, like, all over Insta. Check his hashtag and you'll see. You know he stalks people?' she says as if stalking is a fun thing people might do in their spare time. 'He's so weird.'

What? 'I know Harry, he's my brother, he wouldn't do this!'

Sadie talks slowly to me as if I'm three years old. 'You only know him as a *brother*, you don't know him as a *boyfriend*.'

'And you don't know him at all!' I yell.

I walk off. What does she even mean, know him as a boyfriend? He isn't a boyfriend to anyone! He's never been a boyfriend because he's never had a girlfriend. I don't think. I do remember people saying stuff about him and Amber after that footy match and the drinks in the clubrooms about a month ago. I just ignored it, because she's always going on about some guy or other. And she's always saying how hot Harry is, and she watches them play footy because her brother Sean's in the same team.

Sadie catches up to me. 'You said yourself the other day that he's been acting weird. I mean, how well do you really know him?'

I keep walking. 'He wouldn't do that.'

'Lissa, just look at the post, it has to be him, it makes sense.'

Um, what? 'Actually, Sadie, if you think about it, it *doesn't* make sense. So try thinking about it.'

Wow, I actually knew what to say then.

I can't stop worrying all day at school. Harry couldn't have asked Amber for a nude, then shared that picture. Why would he even do that? To try to impress his friends? It's just not him.

I mean, I feel sorry for Amber that someone's done this to her, but it's not my brother.

We have double science, which I usually like, but I can't focus on the genetics activities. Mrs Tellier even notices, and says, 'Come on, Lissa, where's my keen science student gone? I thought you'd like this prac.'

I try to call Hana, then I message her asking if she's free to facetime later.

And what is Reed doing? When I get home I'll have to deal with him again. This is too much. I need him and Mercy out of my life.

I decide to go to Mum's work after school. I feel helpless, but one thing I can do is ask her. About that email thirteen years ago, and Reed. I told him I would. The sooner I can convince him that my mother has nothing to do with him, the sooner he'll take Mercy and go home. His parents must have called the police by now.

I have to wait for Mum to finish so I head to the hydrotherapy pool, wearing Mum's bathers (too big) because I don't have mine. The pool is basically a huge spa. The water is so warm, almost hot. I lie there trying to take deep breaths and stop thinking about Reed and Mercy. About Harry. After a while I turn the bubbling taps off and sit on the edge. It's so steamy. I can hear Mum working and talking calmly to her clients in the next room. It's a pregnancy Pilates class. I haven't been here for a while. I like going to Mum's work, and not only because of the hydrotherapy pool. I like seeing my mother as a person out in the world, separate from me and Harry. I feel proud of her as she takes the class, organises everyone, gets them moving in the right ways. Competent. It always calms me down.

I can hear bits of what she says. 'Different pregnancies progress differently and feel differently in the body. Watch your back there, shoulders down. Keep your rib to pelvis connection.'

Someone else's voice now, asking a question.

And Mum's answer. 'I've had three pregnancies, each very different.'

Two women come in and turn on the spa. Bubbles start noisily.

Did I just hear that right?

I can't tell them to turn the tap off. They're patients, I'm just the physio's kid.

Three pregnancies?

There are only two of us.

What else don't I know about my mother?

The wind blew her hair right across her face.
She was leaning over, her arm made a loop as she wrote.
Her dress was loose, sheer,

10

DE FACTO

Mum's class is finished. I get dry, and dress back in my school skirt, my shirt and jumper. Everything's hard to get back on when you've been in water.

Sadie has messaged asking if Reed is still there. Technically I don't know if he's still there because I'm not at home so I say that I can't see him so he must have gone back to his parents.

In her office, Mum's looking at her phone. Reading something? A text? The paper? Looking at Insta? Checking her emails? Who knows.

'Mum?'

'Mmmm.'

'Are you sure you don't know someone called Reed Lister?'

She doesn't look up.

'Mum?'

She's distracted, scrolling down her phone in that tired way we all do, not looking at anything properly.

'Reed Lister? Are you sure you don't know him? From, like, years ago?'

Mum stops scrolling and looks at me. 'Reed who?'

'Lister. Reed Lister. Can you please listen?'

'No,' she says, 'I told you the other day, that name doesn't ring a bell.' She goes back to her phone, but an invisible wave has swept over my mother's face, adjusted all her features. She looks somehow younger, almost frightened.

Has she seen something on her phone? Or is it that I mentioned Reed's name again?

Mum unplugs her laptop and puts it in her leather bag. 'Why do you ask?' She's trying to act like it's a casual question, but it feels forced, like a pretend whisper.

'Just a kid at the footy club, someone said he was seeing a physio, I thought you might know him.'

'Sorry, sweets,' she says, putting her phone in her bag, 'he's not one of my patients.' She picks up her bag. 'Let's get going.'

We get in the car. 'Remember Troy's coming for dinner tonight. Very casual,' she adds, 'no need for any fuss,' as if she's literally quoting from Sadie's book about relationships after divorce.

Mum starts the car and reverses out.

'Mum, this is going to sound weird, but you didn't have any other children apart from me and Harry, did you?'

Mum laughs. She's rubbing her shoulder, which she does when she's feeling stressed. She's got this recurring shoulder injury, from a car accident long ago. 'No! Why do you ask me that?'

'No reason.'

The indicator clicks. Mum turns right. 'Strange question to ask for no reason.'

'And I'm not, like, adopted or anything?'

'No, you're not adopted.' She laughs again, shaking her head. 'Why all these questions all of a sudden? Is it because of Dad and Wendy having a baby?'

'Maybe,' I lie. 'That must be it. I have been thinking about that a bit.'

'Is everything okay, Liss?'

'Yep, it's fine.'

'There's only ever been you two, darling. And Dad having another child doesn't change the way he feels about you.'

We stop at the lights.

'Mum, do you reckon Harry's okay?'

'He hasn't got his dad around.'

'Either have I.' And also, we haven't had Dad around for four years.

Maybe she hasn't noticed Harry's been so low and grumpy because she's spending so much time with Troy.

De facto means in fact. Troy might not be married to Mum or anything, but *in fact* he's becoming her partner. De facto. Like no matter what someone says about something, you need to pay attention to the in fact part.

When we get home, Harry's on the couch staring at his laptop. As soon as we walk in, he heads to his room. I look at Mum as if to say, See what I mean?

'I thought you were at training?' says Mum to Harry's back as he's disappearing down the hallway. 'Wasn't Finn's dad going to drop you home? . . . Harry? Where are you playing on Sunday?'

'I'm not.'

'Why not?'

'Because I'm not playing footy.'

'What, this weekend?'

'No. Ever.'

'What? Harry –'

'I didn't tell you because I knew you'd overreact and make a big deal of it. You'd call Dad and then he'd hassle me as well.'

The doorbell rings. 'Okay,' says Mum calmly, 'let's talk about this later. And can you please not be rude to Troy, Harry?'

I need to see where Reed is, but right now I can't do that.

I follow Harry into his bedroom.

I just have to say it, even if it upsets him.

'Sadie showed me something today.'

'The nude?'

I nod. 'On Insta. That Rate Year Eight thing. I know you didn't make that profile.'

'Of course I didn't.'

'Do you know who set it up?'

'I reckon it must be one of the guys from football.'

'Sean? But he's her brother.'

Harry shrugs. 'Robbo, maybe. Liam. Probably a group of them.'

'Amber thinks it's you.' I pause. 'Why would she think that?'

I can't believe I'm asking him this question. 'Did she send you that nude?'

Harry turns away. His back is straight and tall in front of me.

'Did she?'

He nods, still turned away.

'Oh, right.' I'm shocked that she did that, and that he didn't tell me.

'Did you ask her to? Did you send her stuff like that too?'

He turns to face me. 'Of course I didn't. I deleted it as soon as I got it and messaged her to never do something like that again.'

'She thinks you made that profile. Sent that pic around.'

'She could have sent it to other guys as well, not just me. Anyone could have it.'

I sit down on Harry's bed.

'When did all this happen? Like when did it start?' I ask.

'I don't know, about a month ago.' Harry plonks down beside me. 'I don't even know how she had my number. She must have got it off Sean's phone.'

'But why would she even send you that?'

'You know what she's like, hanging around the footy club when they come to pick up Sean, coming into the rooms after games and stuff.'

'She thinks only you had that pic, Harry. That you must have shared it.'

'Well I didn't.'

'You didn't send it to anyone? Not even one person?'

He shakes his head.

'Could someone have got it off your phone?'

'No!' he whisper-shouts. 'I don't have it! I've already told you that!'

'Well, can't you go online and say it wasn't you?'

'Of course I can't. That would stir everything up even more.'

'Have you asked the guys at footy? If they made the profile?'

'They said it wasn't them, but they're all laughing about it. It's probably their idea of a great joke. On both of us, me and Amber. Maybe Sean got that pic off her phone, I don't know.'

'God, why do you have friends like that?'

Harry doesn't answer.

'Did something happen between you and Amber? Did you, like, kiss her or anything? At that party for the coach in the clubrooms?'

'She's in Year Eight! I try to keep away from her. She always comes up to me after footy.'

'Did you, like, flirt with her? Lead her on?'

'I don't think so. I mean we won the game, we were all mucking around, I was just mucking around with Sean.'

'But did you kiss her? Make out?'

'She tried to kiss *me*!'

'Have you seen the comments on the Rate Year Eight post?' I ask.

He holds up his hand. 'Don't tell me. I've heard what they are and I don't want to know.'

'Like what do they mean you have an STD?'

'That's a stupid joke the guys at footy say about me because I hate being in the public showers with them.'

I don't really understand that, and it actually made me feel sick, seeing people write that stuff about my brother. I mean, Harry can be a pain, but he's not all the things that people who don't even know him are saying.

I rest my hand on his shoulder. I realise I haven't touched Harry for a long time. His muscles tense. He's not some random name on social media. He's not every guy who ever did something bad to a girl. He's a warm, living breathing person. One person. My brother.

'I don't know if I ever want to kiss any girl.'

'I'm sure you will.'

'What makes you so sure? You don't know me!'

'I do, Harry.'

And I'm trying to find the words, I think I know what he's trying to say now . . .

'Harry! Lissa!' Mum says fake-brightly. 'Troy's here!'

And here we are at the next meeting – no-fuss, casual dinner.

While Mum's pouring Troy a beer, I head outside.

'Where are you going?' says Harry like he's accusing me of something.

He doesn't care where I'm going, but I don't think he wants to be left alone with Mum and Troy.

'Checking that my sleeping bag's down in the shed. I'll need it when I go to Sadie's place next weekend.' If I keep going down to the shed all the time they'll get suspicious, but I need to see if he's still there, if they're all right.

I open the shed door, step inside.

He's sitting against the metal wall, Mercy in his arms.

'I need to be quick. Don't shine the torch. Everyone's home. Are you okay? Are you warm enough?'

'Mercy's sick. She's been sick again.'

Mercy is whimpering, like she doesn't have the energy to properly cry.

'Should you take her to hospital?'

He shakes his head. 'Can you get some formula? And another banana?'

'I'll try, but it won't be till later, after Troy's gone and Mum's in bed.'

He hands me the bottle with a tiny bit of formula at the bottom.

'And, Reed, I asked her again. My mother doesn't know you. I'm sorry, but this is totally stressing me out. And look at Mercy, she's sick.'

Reed won't look at me. He holds Mercy to him as if someone's trying to take her away.

'Just go home,' I tell him. 'Please.'

I don't know what else to say. I head back up the garden and inside.

Mum is sitting at the kitchen bench with Troy, and Harry is nowhere to be seen. Mum is drinking red wine and Troy has a beer in a can.

'Where's the sleeping bag?' Mum asks.

'Oh, yeah, it's there, I didn't need to get it, but to, um, check where it was.' I stand just inside the back door. Mum looks at me in an odd way. I try to appear less panicked. 'What?' I say.

'It's freezing, Liss, come inside and close that door.' She picks up her phone, she'll be checking her steps. 'I've done over ten thousand today. Well done me!' Mum smiles, trying to relax the tense mood in our house. 'Got to keep moving!'

Mum is always doing stuff, out volunteering. Running free Pilates classes at the commission flats, seeing patients here at home if they can't afford to go to Move Australia, helping kids through The Smith Family, doing the stall at the hospital up the road. 'You don't need to convince everyone that you're a good person,' Harry always tells her.

'What happens if you don't reach ten thousand steps?' Troy asks, smiling too.

'It's not like you self-combust or anything, Mum,' says Harry, loitering in the hallway.

'Harry, there you are! Can you please set the table?'

Harry grabs the cutlery as noisily as he can and kind of drops it on the table. It falls at random angles, so I go and neaten it up a bit.

Mum serves the pasta – gnocchi with meatballs and tomato sauce – and we sit at the table in the back room.

'This is delicious, Fi,' says Troy. He's made a dessert – apple crumble, and he's brought Maggie Beer ice-cream as well. The salted honey and almond one. Mum never buys it because it's so expensive.

'Troy was in the paper yesterday, for the bravery medal,' says Mum. We know about his bravery medal because Mum went to see him get it from the premier. It was last month, before Harry and I met Troy. He got it for rescuing a seven-year-old girl in a rip at Fairhaven. When Mum got home from the award ceremony she was smiling more than ever, which made me think at the time that she must be pretty keen on this Troy guy.

'The journalist called it hysterical strength,' says Mum.

'I don't think so,' says Troy. 'The kid was in trouble. I mean, it was a tough swim, but it was doable.'

'She said we draw on extreme strength in life and death situations.'

'Like those clips on YouTube where mothers lift cars off their kids,' I say.

Harry moves gnocchi around his plate. He usually eats everything, really quickly.

Okay, that topic's done.

Mum tries again. 'Troy's been working this week in Gippsland. On the way to the prom.'

Silence. I remember one time we camped there, we found a dead kangaroo on the road with a live joey in her pouch. Mum wrapped the joey in a shopping bag, and we drove two hours with it to the animal rescue place.

'I told Troy that we've been camping there.'

'Yeah, when Dad was around,' mutters Harry, and Troy looks uncomfortable, takes a mouthful of beer.

It's like Mum's interviewing the three of us. Poor Mum, it's so tense, and I can't focus on anything she's talking about because I'm too worried about Harry, and about Reed. But I'm also trying to think of something to say. Something that's light-hearted and won't lead to Harry being mean to me, or to Mum, or to Troy.

'Hey, we did this thing in science today.'

'What was that, Liss?' Mum seems so relieved that one of her children is contributing to the conversation.

'I'll show you. Hang on, I need to finish my mouthful.' I take a gulp of water.

'What are you doing with your tongue?'

'Gross!'

I roll my tongue into a perfect circle. 'Can you do it?'

Harry eventually tries, but he can't. People look funny trying to roll their tongue or go cross-eyed or do that thing when one eyebrow goes up and one goes down. Basically you can do these things or you can't.

'Can you, Mum?'

'No.'

Troy tries. He can!

'It's so easy!' I say. 'For me, too.'

It does relax the mood a bit because it's hard not to smile when someone makes a ridiculous face.

'Dad must be able to do it, then,' I say. 'It's inherited. Like blue and brown eyes. Recessive and dominant genes. It was actually really interesting. I'll ask Dad tomorrow when we see him.'

'Are you sure that's not a wives' tale?' Troy says. 'The tongue thing?'

'Look,' says Mum, quite crossly almost, 'it's an oversimplified genetic trait. Not scientifically accurate.' Then she changes the subject.

'How was the new car, going down to Gippsland?'

'Good! Really nice to drive.'

Mum turns to us. 'Troy's got a new car. A Toyota.'

Troy nods. 'Hilux.'

Troy's got this, Troy's done that. She really wants us to like him.

Harry looks up from his gnocchi, shows like one speck of interest. He's always hassling Mum to take him driving so he can get his hours up. He got his Learner's the day after his sixteenth birthday. But she's totally a back-seat driver. She gets so stressed.

'Automatic or manual?'

'Manual,' says Troy. Then, 'Hey,' he says, 'do you have your Learner's?'

'Yep, but I haven't done much driving,' says Harry. 'Because whenever we go, *someone* goes psycho.'

'That's not true,' says Mum. 'I'm a careful driver. I'm happy to take you, it's just that it always seems to end in an argument.'

'She's more than careful,' Harry turns to Troy, 'she's a nervous driver. And she hates freeways. It's easy to drive on a freeway. Sometimes she'll jam on her brakes for no reason, nothing there.'

'I said I'm happy to take you,' repeats Mum.

'Don't worry about it, Mum,' Harry puts salad on his plate, 'I'll get someone else to do it.'

'I will,' says Troy.

We all look at him. Troy's smart, I think. Harry won't be able to resist this.

'I'll take you driving. We can go after dinner, if it's okay with your mum. Just up the street, maybe the Bunnings carpark, for half an hour or so. We can take the Hilux, or we could start with your mum's Golf.'

'Okay,' says Harry slowly, as if Troy has challenged him to a duel.

'Have you got L plates?'

'Are you sure?' asks Mum. 'It's dark.'

'I need to drive at night, too,' says Harry.

She looks at Troy, and I think her look says thanks.

They decide to do the driving first and then come back for dessert.

While they're out, we rinse the plates and put them in the dishwasher. Troy's apple crumble is in the oven. The kitchen smells of vanilla and cinnamon.

'Do you think Harry's really given up football?' I ask Mum.

'I'd be very surprised.' Mum wipes the kitchen bench and checks her phone. I check mine too. Nothing from Hana, but she's put up an Insta story of all her new, suntanned friends jumping off a jetty into the blue sea, screaming and laughing.

'I got a message from Amber's mother,' says Mum. 'She texted me yesterday as well but I haven't had a minute to get back to her.' Mum glances at her phone again. 'Now she says it's urgent. Do you have any idea what that's about?'

I place a knife neatly beside another knife on the top tray of the dishwasher. 'No.'

'Probably the boys and football. I'll call her in the morning. I'll try to get a bit more out of Harry first.'

'She might have wanted you to give Sean a lift home from training.'

'True, she often asks me to do that. And she always says it's urgent.'

'Yeah, so does Amber.'

Mum's laughing to herself. 'Come and look at this, Liss.'

We look at the text chain with Amber's mother. All her texts start with *Hi Fiona, I'm going to need*.

> I'm going to need you to pick Sean up from training
>
> I'm going to need you to take Sean to the match. Urgent!
>
> I'm going to need you to do my timekeeping roster.
> Sorry urgent.

> I'm going to need you to have Sean on Friday night

> I'm going to need you to give Sean dinner after the
> game. It's urgent.

It's like the chorus of a song, like that Proclaimers song,
'I'm Gonna Be'.

Occasionally she needs Mum to do something with Amber
(*I'm going to need you to have Amber after netball*) but I think
she usually asks other people, like Sadie's mum, rather than
my mum. Amber wouldn't want to hang out with me all the
time, but Sean and Harry are quite good friends.

Amber's mother, Lorraine, is very busy. She runs a pram-
cleaning business. First Class Prams. She doesn't do any of the
cleaning, she runs the whole business and they have franchises
all over Australia. My mum and Amber's mum are like total
opposites. Except that they're both fit. Amber's mum is loud and
dramatic. My mum is calmer, she doesn't like being the centre
of attention. Amber's mum's always travelling, my mum likes
being at home. And Amber's stepdad is as old as a grandfather.
That's another thing they don't have in common. Amber's
mum – ancient, rich boyfriend who wears dark sunglasses
with gold on the sides, pale pink shirts and leather slip-on
shoes, and drives Amber to school in his Porsche convertible.
My mum – young boyfriend who wears tradie shorts and
Blundstones and drives a Toyota Hilux. Lol.

'You didn't tell me you were sleeping over at Sadie's next
weekend. That's good, are you becoming better friends?'

'Kind of. I suppose.'

'And with Amber?'

'I don't really like Amber much.'

'Mmm,' says Mum.

'I miss Hana.'

'I know you do, Liss.'

I see light down in the garden under the shed door. Turn the torch off! I yell in my mind to Reed.

Mum hands me the salad bowl to put away. 'Are you okay? You seem a bit distant. Are you okay with me and Troy? I know it's an adjustment.'

I'm so fine with Mum and Troy, but I have a boy and a baby hiding out in the shed in the back garden. And a brother who I think is being trolled on social media. I want to tell Mum but I can't.

'Year Eight's a tough year,' she says.

'Yeah, everyone's in their groups.'

'Can't you be in a group?'

'I'm kind of in a group. But they always do what Amber tells them to do, or what they think she wants them to do. Like they can't even choose their own friends. And they believe whatever she tells them. I reckon Amber doesn't like me because she thinks I want to be friends with Sadie.'

'Do you? Want to be Sadie's friend?'

I shrug. 'I don't know. Sometimes. Not really.'

I suppose I'm just lonely at school now.

'Have you heard from Hana lately?' Mum asks.

'Hana doesn't message me like she used to. We've lost our streak.' I dry a saucepan. 'I always thought we'd be friends for life.'

'You still might be,' says Mum. 'By the way, I spoke to Rachel yesterday, she wants us to check the garden on the weekend. I collected the key from the house-sitter, she's left the place in a bit of a mess.' Rachel is Hana's mum, she's friends with my mum.

'You know, it's one of the nice things about growing up,' says Mum, hanging a tea towel on the hook. 'You get to choose your friends, make your own friendship group.'

I think of the friends Mum and Dad had before they separated. Family friends of ours, too. Some stayed with Mum, some with Dad, some stayed friends with both, some drifted away. And then there are new friends. Like Troy.

'A friendship group has a life,' says Mum. 'A beginning, a middle and an end. And individual friends, too. You know the old saying – a friend is for a reason, a season or a lifetime.' Mum's putting a protein bar in her lunch bag for tomorrow. She gets an apple from the fruit bowl. 'Who keeps eating the bananas? I suppose if Harry eats them all then it's his problem if there are none left for breakfast.'

Harry's on a special diet because his coach told him he has to put on four kilos if he wants to train with the Eastern Rangers. But maybe he won't do that now, if he's given up footy like he says.

'I ate a couple yesterday,' I tell Mum.

Harry and Troy come in, they're chatting in a friendly way, like two men together, then Harry actually says thank you for the drive.

'How did you get on?' Mum asks.

'Fine,' says Troy. 'Harry's a good driver.'

Troy gets the apple crumble out of the oven and Mum serves it. I can taste the vanilla bean, and the apples have gone a bit caramelised. Delicious.

'I bet Mum didn't buy this,' says Harry when he sees the high-end ice-cream. He eats heaps of it.

Mum and Troy have a cup of tea sitting at the kitchen bench. Harry goes to his room and I'm sitting there not knowing if I should go to my room too, or hang around. I keep looking down towards the shed. The light is off. I hope they're okay.

Sometimes we watch the footy on a Friday night, but maybe Mum wants to avoid this because of Harry saying he's giving it up.

Then Mum says that she wants to watch a program on iview about the wellness industry. 'A colleague at work recommended it. Want to stay and watch it?' she asks Troy casually. 'Or would you rather watch the game?'

'Happy to watch your program,' says Troy.

I feel rude going to my bedroom, so I sit with them. It's like they decide to not sit too close together on the couch. It's quite funny, they're both sitting up neatly making sure no part of them is touching the other person.

'The wellness industry is growing globally and is worth 4.2 trillion dollars,' says the voiceover while we watch people running and doing yoga and tai chi.

There's all the normal things like Pilates and mindfulness, but there's also wellness tourism, wellness real estate, and something called the spa economy. There's even a 'sound bath' where people lie down and 'consume sound'. It's called 'sound healing'. Someone hits a gong and it echoes and resonates for a long time afterwards.

At the end of the show, the smiling woman says, 'And the good news is, with the rise of an ageing population, chronic disease, stress and unhappiness, there is only growth for the wellness industry!'

'I suppose that's a good thing?' says Mum.

'Does it need to be an industry?' Troy smiles. 'Eat well, exercise, get sleep, be with people you love. It's not that hard.' He stands up. 'I better be off. Got an early start in the morning.'

Troy's right, it shouldn't be that complicated to be well.

Mum says goodbye to him, then goes out to put the beer cans in the recycling. I take the Maggie Beer tub from the freezer and eat the last of the ice-cream.

Maybe it's the syrupy, creamy nuttiness of the ice-cream, maybe it's the wellness show, or maybe it's that Troy seems like an uncomplicated, decent person, someone who doesn't make things difficult, and a bit of that must have rubbed off on me, because I think, kind of suddenly, that everything might be okay. Like I'm answering that question at the end of all my lists. Harry could go on Insta and explain that he had nothing to do with Rate Year Eight, and next week there might be a new Insta drama for everyone to get obsessed with. And I might have been reading that look of my mum's all wrong, and Reed's Fiona Freeman is just some random person who is nothing to do with my mother. And Reed did say he is prepared to go home tomorrow. I taste the dark salty honey on my tongue. And maybe it's only a stage with Hana, and when I see her again, everything will be like it was. And when I'm older I can make my own friendship group. Maybe I heard wrong about the third pregnancy. Maybe it's like what that TV show said about mindfulness. We've done it at school, too. We have to practise letting the anxious feelings come and go, observe them like suitcases on a conveyer belt at the airport. They come, they go past us. Maybe I'm catastrophising, and everything's not as bad as I think it is.

But my suitcase on the conveyer belt is about to come around.

Mum comes and sits on the couch. 'I think I can hear a baby crying.'

'I can't hear anything,' I say, too quickly.

Mum puts a hand on my thigh, turns down the TV with the remote, tilts her head. 'Listen.'

Anyone could hear it.

I look at Mum. Oh god. I'll have to say something . . .

'The Fyfields must have their daughter and her baby staying with them,' says Mum. She pats my knee, leans back on the couch. 'Thank you for sitting with us and watching that program.'

Phew. 'No worries, Mum.' I try to sound relaxed but my tummy feels twisted. Mercy, please stop! I need to get back down to the shed with that last bit of formula. But I need Mum to go to bed first. Eventually she goes to the bathroom.

I get up to turn the TV off, but the nine-thirty newsbreak comes on.

'In breaking news, police hold concerns for a thirteen-year-old boy, Reed Lister, who has been missing for three days from his home in Ballarat. He was last seen in Main Street, Ballarat, on Monday but it is believed he may have made his way to Melbourne. He has not been active on social media or accessed his bank account. He requires medication to be taken every day. If anyone has any information about his whereabouts, please contact Crime Stoppers on –'

I feel my face go hot, the last of the ice-cream melts to nothing in my mouth. Has Mum heard it?

I turn the TV off, and google Reed's name on my phone. There's no more information, except a picture of Reed and his parents. They look happy. His parents look old-fashioned, like they could be from the 1970s or something. Reed's hair is different in the photo. There's nothing about him being adopted, or a medical condition. What medical condition? Is Reed sick as well as Mercy?

Mum's gone into Harry's room. I can hear her talking quietly to him. She's probably asking about what's happening with football. The sound of Mercy's crying is sweeping up our back garden like it's a valley. Mum's laptop is in her leather bag sitting on the table in the back room. I grab it.

'Let's talk about it tomorrow then,' I hear Mum say, and she's coming back so I shove the laptop back in her bag.

She stands at the door. 'That was nice, wasn't it, Liss? Dinner with Troy?'

'Yep, it was nice,' I say, because it actually was. Until five minutes ago.

Mum goes down the hall and I hear the shower running. I grab the laptop again from her bag and open it. I look through the emails, scrolling, scrolling. Physio appointments, an email from Dad about tomorrow, a Telstra bill. Feels like I'm eavesdropping. I suppose I am. Book Depository. Webjet. The

Conversation. Nothing from Reed Lister, and nothing sent to him either. I do a search for his name, and Foster Families, too. Nothing.

I'm about to close it when I see the bin in the left-hand panel of Mail. My hand moves across and I left click. 2XU ads, Kogan, Pinterest, all the stuff she deletes.

And an email.

Reed Lister, 6.41 pm, 3 June 2019.

I double-click.

> Dear Fiona Freeman,
> Sorry if this is a shock to you. My name is Reed Lister. This week I found out that I am adopted. I have an email from 2006 written by someone with your name, and I want to know if it's you. I don't want money or anything, I only want to know who my birth parents are. I think you could help me. Are you my mother? Please reply to this email address. Thank you.
> Sincerely,
> Reed Lister

It was the right email.

The right address.

To the right Fiona Freeman.

I close the laptop.

*Leaning, leaning, then
she fell.*

11

LULLABY

At last Mum goes to bed. 11.07 pm. Sadie has messaged me.

> That guy was on the news. Amber and me are
> going to call crimestoppers.

Me:

> No need. He's gone. On his way home.

And one from Poppy, which I think is about Harry, not Reed.

> I believe Amber.

Me:

> You shouldn't believe everything she says.

Poppy:

> Sorry I'm on Amber's team.

Since when were there teams?

I need to tell Reed about that email, and the TV news. I boil the water, mix the formula, make the bottle, and head down to the shed. Mercy has stopped crying. There's no moon but the clouds are an eerie orange colour.

Girls from school sneak out at night all the time. They take their parents' alcohol and go down to the park to meet friends and get drunk. They come back at like 5 am. I'm sneaking out too. I don't care if Mum wakes up and freaks out if I'm not in my room. She's not being honest with me, so why should I care about her feelings right now?

Reed and Mercy are both asleep. Mercy is wheezing, hiccupping like she's cried herself to sleep, and doing that raggedy breathing. I feel worried for both of them. What's the medication that Reed's supposed to take?

I hold the bottle, it warms up my hands. I stand there, staring down at them.

It's like Reed is looking after Mercy, and I'm looking after Reed.

You know when someone comes into your room when you're asleep, even if they're really quiet, you sense it and you wake up.

'Hey, Lissa.'

'Hi. Did you get some sleep?'

'I'm scared I'll squash her if I fall asleep,' he says, holding Mercy gently in his arms.

'Let's not wake her up,' I whisper. The night is so still, so quiet, the sound would really travel.

But too late, she's going to start crying again.

I give Reed the bottle. 'It's too hot for her,' he says.

'I didn't know she'd be drinking it right away.' He could have said thank you for getting it! No one appreciates what I'm doing for them. I go to the tap in the garden. Dark, icy water runs over my hands as I top up the bottle. I'm sure a bit of tap water won't hurt her.

'Feel her forehead,' whispers Reed when I come back in.

My hand covers her whole forehead because she's so tiny. 'It's hot.'

'But her hands are cold.'

'Better give her this.'

Mercy starts drinking.

'Hey, Reed?'

He looks up.

'My mum did get your email. The one you sent to that old Yahoo address the other day. I found it tonight, in the bin of her mail. That old address must still be active, even though it's not the one she uses. It's hers. Which means she must be the Fiona Freeman who sent that email to your parents thirteen years ago.'

Reed nods like he's not that surprised.

'But she doesn't want me to know about it,' I add.

'I need to speak with her,' Reed says. 'She can help me.'

'I asked her twice and she said she doesn't know you. She's hiding something, but what is it? And also, Reed, you were on the news, the TV. Just before. I saw it. You're a missing person. It said to contact Crime Stoppers.'

'Shit.'

'That's what I thought. The police could come here, tonight.'

Mercy doesn't want any more of the bottle. She's struggling in Reed's arms and looks like she might start crying again. Reed holds the dummy to her mouth. The dummy does seem to help a bit, but Mercy always spits it out. It lands on the dirt floor and he brushes it off on the sleeping bag and puts it back in her mouth, holds it in. She sucks on it.

'Did they mention Mercy? On the news?'

'No, but Sadie saw it and messaged me that she's going to call the police. She will have told Amber, too. Everyone will be looking for you. You need to let your parents know you're safe. Reed, you're a missing person. They might think you've been kidnapped, or anything. Murdered! And I'll get in trouble as well. For hiding you and Mercy.'

'How can I do this to them?' Reed pleads to me as if I might have a reasonable answer to this question. 'I'm their good child.' He pushes his glasses back up his nose, which is tricky because he's also holding Mercy and the dummy in her mouth. His glasses must have got loose. 'I'm the one who doesn't let them down, who they never have to worry about. It was so stupid that they never told me, but I've been sitting here thinking about it, and I can almost understand why they didn't.' His glasses have slid down again, and he looks over them at me like a judge in a movie. 'Given the circumstances.'

I sit down beside Reed on a crate. 'Can I have a bit of sleeping bag?'

He moves so I can pull some of it my way.

'Let's try the bottle again.'

Mercy drinks now.

'Like, they might think it would jeopardise me, upset my life,' says Reed.

'Parents must have whole complicated and stupid reasons for doing the things that they do,' I tell him. I don't think any parent actually intends to stuff everything up.

'They worry about me now, too. Since I've started high school.'

'What about?'

'My politics.'

I almost laugh. The way he says it, as if he's one of those super-extreme vegans who goes around kidnapping farm animals.

'I went on strike that day.'

'Yeah, you told me . . . Thousands of kids, of people, did, I did too.'

'I got the train down from Ballarat. They didn't want me to. They're so . . . frightened. That I might turn out like Eliot. Or something.' He puts Mercy's dummy back in, holds it gently in her mouth. I think Mercy might be too young for a dummy. She doesn't seem to get it. 'It's like they have some kind of rope that they're gripping, and they're praying that it'll hold, that they won't have to let go.'

'Do they actually pray?'

'Yeah,' says Reed. 'That's why they don't care about climate change. They put their trust in God.'

'Then can't they put their trust in God where Eliot's concerned?' I ask.

Reed thinks for a moment. 'Eliot's not the kind of son my father wanted. He wanted a different son.'

'Like you?'

'Not me.' Reed shakes his head. 'They don't like the way I stress about everything. Climate change, terrorism, pandemics, and, like, 9/11. They think that God will sort everything out. But do you know how many people died in 9/11? Do you know that some of them jum—'

'Yeah, I know, I've seen the footage,' I say.

'And they knew they were going to die and they had to text their families to say goodbye.'

'Yeah.'

Then I remind him. 'You need to text *your* family, Reed.'

We both look down at little Mercy, sucking on the dummy that Reed's holding in her mouth. Drifting in and out of sleep.

'What are you going to do with her?'

'What am I supposed to do! I thought Eliot would help me, not hand me his baby and tell me to take her!'

'Can't someone try to find Mercy's mother?'

'There's no point. Sienna's got more problems than Eliot.'

'Oh, right.' I stand up and bounce on my toes because I'm totally freezing. There used to be some other sleeping bags, maybe Mum threw them out, they were like cheap ones for little kids. I'm looking over in the corner of the shed, I lift up the drop sheets we use for painting, and something is glinting there. It's a bottle. 'Hey, can you shine the torch on this?'

Vodka.

'Is this yours?'

'No.'

'It's not mine.' It must be Harry's. Another thing I don't know about him.

I hold it up to see how much is left. 'Have you ever tasted vodka?'

Reed shakes his head. 'My parents don't drink,' he says as if that answers the question.

I've tasted Dad's beer, and once I tasted a cocktail when we were on holidays. I didn't like either. I open the bottle.

'Maybe don't,' says Reed.

'I just want a taste.' I take a sip. Disgusting. I pass it to Reed. 'No,' he says, as he's lifting it to his lips and taking a sip, too. He screws up his face. I don't think he likes it either, it's so yuck but it does feel like it's warming me up a bit.

'I think it's making me feel warmer,' I say.

'That's a myth,' says Reed, handing back the bottle. 'We should put it away. Alcohol doesn't raise your body temperature. It dehydrates you.'

I remember learning something about that at school, too. I take another mouthful. It tastes so bad! How could people skol it!

'My brother must have hidden it here,' I say. I want to tell Reed about Harry, but Reed has enough going on right now. 'I shouldn't have any more,' he says as if he's an adult at a party who's had three glasses of wine. 'I'm responsible for a baby.'

I put the bottle back under the drop sheets.

'Eliot can't manage Mercy now, but he might when he gets better,' Reed says. 'Mum and Dad always said he'd grow out of it, it was difficult teenage years. But now he's nineteen and he's not growing out of it, he's growing into it. If someone could look after her until he gets better . . .'

'They said on the news that you have a medical condition. You require medication every day.'

'That's only because I can't sleep, ever since Eliot left. It's got worse since Mercy was born. I worry about her a lot, but I couldn't tell anyone. I messaged Eliot every day but he hardly ever responded. I went there when I could, but it was only like three times and even then I had to lie. It was really hard.'

I sit down again, pull a bit of the sleeping bag up over my knees.

'Also I think I have climate change anxiety,' Reed continues. 'Eco anxiety. But I don't need the medication the doctor gave me. I don't even take it, I throw it away, my parents don't know that. They think worrying about something that's actually destroying the planet is a disease! A medical condition. They made me see this doctor, and now I'm not supposed to read anything about climate change for two hours before bed. Then I lie there thinking about bushfires, and when I try to stop that, I imagine our recycling bin sitting in our driveway, that the council doesn't know what to do with now that China isn't accepting our recyclable waste.' He gets more agitated. 'Like not reading about it isn't going to help me, or the actual problem!'

'Calm down, Reed,' I say. 'Your voice is too loud.'

He takes a couple of deep breaths. Maybe he does meditation at school, too. 'Sorry.' He lowers his voice. 'Basically, sometimes I can't sleep because of climate change, sometimes I can't sleep because of terrorism, like 9/11, and sometimes I can't sleep because I'm worrying about Mercy. And Eliot.'

I should tell Reed about the fluidised bed combustion system that they have in Japan to burn their waste and then use the heat to create power. Wendy told me all about it because she's worked in Tokyo. But right now I'm worried about the police coming to our house in the middle of the night.

'If Sadie's called the police, they'll come here. Amber's mum might have seen it, too. Or Amber might have told her. Anyone who knows at school could have called the police if they saw it on TV. It might have been on the news online. It's not safe for you and Mercy here now.'

'But your mum wrote that email! She knows something! If she's not going to tell you anything, who else can we ask?'

'I've been thinking about that. Dad must know something. I can ask him, I'm seeing him tomorrow. But I'm scared the police will come here tonight, looking for you.' I wonder if Reed has broken any laws. Would they arrest him? And take Mercy away?

'Where can I go?'

'I don't know, Reed!' Why does he ask me these questions! Actually, then I did know.

'Hana's place is empty. You know my friend who's gone back to WA? They had a house-sitter but she's left. Mum collected the spare key from her for Hana's mum. Omigod, we've got the key! You can go inside and sleep there, in Hana's bed if you like!'

'Do they have an alarm?'

'Oh yeah, they do.' Not such a great idea after all. 'But hang on, you can get in using the key and then turn the alarm off. The code's on the keyring. Take the sleeping bags. The power will be off but at least you'll be inside.'

'Okay, then.' Reed struggles to stand up while holding Mercy. The roof is low, it's lucky we're both small people.

'Want me to hold her?'

But he's okay.

'It would be good to have a pram,' he says, looking around as if one might suddenly appear.

'We don't have a pram!' What does he think this shed is? Kmart?

He hands me the bottle and the last of the formula. I go back inside. The kettle's still warm so I don't re-boil it because I'm scared it might wake Mum. I don't put the light on either, I mix Mercy's bottle by the light of my phone. It's like Reed and I are playing some game where we're parents of a baby. I take the spare key to Hana's place from the kitchen drawer. What am I even doing? Turning into some kind of criminal? I hope Hana's mum and dad would understand. I grab one of Jo's blankets from the couch. Maybe we can make a sling for Reed to carry Mercy in.

As I get near the shed again, I don't hear crying, but something else. It's Reed, singing softly. I realise after a moment that he's singing that My Chemical Romance song, 'I'm Not Okay', which is a very weird choice of lullaby. Still, when Reed sings it slowly in his husky half-broken voice, like acapella, it's a sweet, sad sound.

I open the shed door. 'Look, she's not crying,' Reed says. 'She's calm now, from the singing. She likes it. It's Eliot's favourite song.'

'That's really good. Nice work, Reed.'

But this isn't a time for lullabies. I need to get him out of here. Oh god, what will happen to them? To me? I mean, it's the police!

'She feels a bit weak in my arms. Limp.'

I hold up the blanket. 'Let's make a sling for her.' Crouching and freezing in the shed, we YouTube 'baby slings' and follow the instructions. We do our best with the folding and tying and crossing over. It doesn't look much like the ones on YouTube, but it'll do.

I put the bottle in his backpack. 'Give her this when she wakes up again.'

'We might need to get some more formula.'

'No, because you're going home tomorrow.'

'But now we know your mum knows something about me. Like she could be my moth—'

'Reed, she's not your mother.'

'A relative, then. Someone . . . I can't go home yet!' He's standing very near to me. 'She knows something! This is my only chance.' The steel of his glasses glints, his eyes are open wide. He grabs my arm. 'I feel like we're so close. To finding something. And you're seeing your dad tomorrow.'

'Don't come back here then,' I say quickly. 'I'll come to Hana's place tomorrow once I've seen Dad. We're seeing them in the morning. I don't know what time I'll come.' If no one's going to be honest with me then I might just show Mum that email sitting in her bin and see what she says.

I hand Reed the key. 'Stay inside Hana's house and don't go anywhere.'

'Sorry I've made you worry too,' he says.

I sigh. I feel a lot older than him right now. 'That's okay, Reed, you go to Hana's place now. Have you got paper in your backpack? I'll draw you a map of where to go.'

'I know it,' he says. 'The second street we passed on the way to Chemist Warehouse? Sesame Street.'

'Number fourteen. With a white fence. You've got a good sense of direction.'

We prop my phone on a pile of storage tubs so we can see by the torch, and we get Mercy into the sling without dropping her or waking her up, which we're pretty pleased about. It's a bit low so I try to tighten it by adjusting the crossed bits of the knitted rug across Reed's back. I have to really stretch it.

We leave the shed as quietly as we can.

'Actually, I have a terrible sense of direction,' he tells me. 'I need to focus very hard on where I am. And where other things are. That's how I manage.'

We reach the top of the driveway. 'Okay, well, bye,' we whisper to each other, and Reed sets off down the street, walking into the night.

I stand there for a moment, still tasting the sour, burning feeling of the vodka in my throat. Under the streetlight, Reed turns and waves. I wave back, but I don't know if he sees that.

Jo's rug is too big for a sling. It's hanging down, almost dragging on the road, bright coloured squares on the cold black asphalt. I see Mercy's little head lolling to one side as Reed trudges in and out from streetlight to dark, the weight of the sling making him stoop.

I head back inside. Harry's phone is charging on the kitchen bench. It's like the one rule of our house, to leave our phones out here when we go to sleep. Half the time we don't do it which makes Mum mad. I know his password, it's such a stupid one. 3456. Harry doesn't seem to care, maybe he's even forgotten that I know it.

What is happening to me? I don't keep secrets, I never spy on people . . . I tap in the password and scroll down. No messages from Amber. No text chain. I go to photos. There aren't many, he doesn't take many. Nothing.

I go to Recently Deleted.

The nude is there.

Underneath it says twenty-eight days. Photos stay in Recently Deleted for thirty days.

Harry deleted it two days ago.

There might be new laws in the future, but how will police arrest every bully on social? Anyone who shares something that isn't true? It's basically a huge uncontrolled experiment we're in. I don't know how, but change has to come from us.

SATURDAY

12

SOLSTICE

The shortest day of the year.

I get up when it's still dark because I want to go to Hana's to see Reed before Mum gets up. I notice that Harry's phone isn't on the bench.

I should tell Hana that I'm using her house as a hideout for a runaway and a baby but it feels like we don't have that type of friendship anymore. And also, her parents might be really mad. It could put Hana in a difficult position, knowing what I've done.

I get a message. From Sadie.

> Have the police come yet?

And then one from Hana.

> OMG did your brother really make that profile?

This. From Hana? My friend? And Harry's friend, too. Why doesn't she call him Harry in this message? Not 'your brother', as if she doesn't even know him. Doesn't she remember when the kids at school were teasing her little brother Eli because he couldn't kick the footy, and Harry spent hours in the backyard with him, showing him how to do it? Doesn't she remember that?

I throw my phone on the carpet. Phones! I hate them!

I hear Mum getting up, so I can't leave the house to see Reed. I'm in the kitchen making toast when Mum comes in. She kisses me, puts the kettle on.

'I called Lorraine back last night. She has some story about seeing you with a young man and a baby a couple of days ago? You said he was your cousin?'

I spread butter across my toast, it's melting as I go. Sounds like Lorraine doesn't know about the TV news. Or didn't when she spoke to Mum. But she must know now. I look over at Mum's phone on the bench. Has Lorraine texted her?

'Are you seeing a boy that you don't want us to know about?'

'No, Mum!'

But then I think, Great, let them think that and then I won't have to say any more. So I smile, and Mum says, 'That's nice if you're seeing a boy. No need to be so coy about it. Although Lorraine did say that he'd run away. That he was from the country somewhere.'

'Mum, you know how overdramatic she is. And Amber makes up a heap of stuff.'

Mum still looks worried. 'Is there something you're not telling me?'

Is she wondering how I know the name Reed Lister?

'No.' I sit at the bench with my toast. I actually feel like asking her the same question.

'Are you coming with us today, Mum?'

Dad and Wendy are picking us up at ten-thirty.

'No.'

I must look concerned because then she says, 'Don't worry, Liss, they invited me.'

'What will you do, then?' I hope she's not going to check on Hana's house. Reed has to get out of there before that. 'Hey, can you wait for me to go and check on Hana's place?' I ask.

'Sure. Or we can go tomorrow if you like. This morning I'll go for a run and . . . things.'

I bet she's meeting Troy for coffee or breakfast or something.

'Does Dad know about Harry and football?'

'I texted him about it, suggested he have a chat with him.'

I have a shower, get dressed, pick up my stupid phone.

Another message from Sadie.

> You lied.

> You said he'd gone back.

Then everyone is messaging me. If they didn't see it on TV, then Sadie and Amber have told them.

Sadie again.

> No offence but you're so weird, you're always doing weird things.

Then another message.

> I don't really want to be friends with a weirdo. With a creepy brother. Just my personal opinion.

I respond.

> Amber is lying about my brother. He never led her on never used her.

Sadie:

> You're the liar.
>
> He made her send him that nude, he shared it.
>
> It's not only Amber saying it. It's everyone.
>
> She asked him to take it down but he won't.

Me:

> How can he take it down if he didn't put it up? He's got nothing to do with RateYear8.

But I know he only deleted the pic two days ago. I need to talk to Harry but Mum is hanging around and Harry hogs the bathroom for ages. When he gets out it's almost ten past ten. I follow him straight into his bedroom. He's standing there, still dripping from the shower, with a towel around his waist.

'Can you get out?' he says. 'Can I get dressed please?'

I close the door behind me.

'Lissa, can I get dressed now? Dad'll be here in a minute.'

'Harry . . .'

'What?'

'I saw it on your phone. The nude. I'm sorry I looked. I only saw that one photo. I was worried.'

'But I deleted it!'

'Yeah, like two days ago. It was still in Recently Deleted.'

'Shit,' whispers Harry. He grabs his phone and deletes it permanently.

Then he stops, stares out the window, his shoulders fall, he has a man's body but he's not a man. He's a kid, like me. He gets a t-shirt from the drawer, pulls it over his head.

'Okay, I didn't delete it when I got it. But it's gone now. And can you not look at my phone? Jesus, Lissa.'

He opens his cupboard and takes a hoodie from a hanger.

'Why did you tell me you deleted it as soon as you got it?'

No answer.

'Harry, I want to believe you, I do believe you, but –'

The doorbell rings.

Mum opens the bedroom door.

Dad and Wendy are here.

It's actually a relief to see Dad. I remember when things were simpler. He hugs me and kisses the top of my head. I only realise how much I miss him when I see him. Since he's been with Wendy he's lost weight, and he uses product in his hair, which is grey but he has a cooler haircut now too. And he wears some kind of male fragrance. I can smell it. He looks more like Harry, or maybe it's that Harry is looking more like Dad these days. Harry, Mum and Dad are all tall and really strong, and I'm strong too, but I'm small. Slight. I don't really look like Dad at all.

Mum kisses Wendy and says hi to Dad. It's strange that two people who once loved each other, who lived together for years, are now just polite like they hardly know each other. But they never say anything bad about each other to me or Harry.

I don't think Mum wanted to come with us. I suppose it would be pretty strange going out with your ex and his wife – even though they all get on fine, and Mum really likes Dad's sister, our aunty Jo, who we're meeting at the restaurant.

Wendy is very pregnant now.

'You look great,' says Mum. 'How many weeks?'

Wendy looks as if she's about to have the baby, but it's not due for like two months. 'I've been doing the Pilates,' she says, with her hand on her tummy.

'Good.' Mum smiles. 'I think it's very helpful.'

We go to a yum cha restaurant in the city that Dad likes. It's funny, he lives in China, you'd think he'd choose another cuisine when he's here.

On the way I keep looking over at Harry, trying to catch his eye, but he's staring out the window. Poor Harry. Whatever he has or hasn't done, I still feel sorry for him. When we pass Hana's street, I don't look up towards her house. I can't even think about Reed right now. The car radio's on but I want it off, I don't want to hear any news. I wonder if the police will go to our place this morning, while I'm out. What will they say to Mum?

The restaurant is a big place, noisy and bustling. Jo's there already, sitting at a round table with a red tablecloth which matches her hair. She stands up. She's wearing a very colourful coat. Jo's an interior designer, she specialises in something called colour forecasting. Her business card actually says Joanna Freeman, Colour Forecaster.

'Look at you, Harry! You're huge!'

Jo hasn't seen us for about three months. She plonks her bag from the seat next to her onto the floor. 'You sit here, next to me,' she tells Harry.

'Wendy, Wendy, WENDY!'

'Yes, that's her name,' says Harry under his breath. But Wendy is laughing and holding both of Jo's hands in her own.

As soon as we sit down, the trolleys are wheeled by. The waitresses look bored as they lift the bamboo lids, asking us if we want prawn dumplings, fried bean curd, steamed pork buns, sticky rice? Dad says yes to everything, even chicken feet and fish-head soup. My tummy feels churned up before we start eating, and after twenty minutes we're all full, but we keep eating because the trolleys keep coming and the food is so delicious.

I want to stop thinking about everything that's worrying me. I try to imagine the suitcases, the worries coming and going. I need to tell Reed that method, it might help him with his climate change anxiety. But actually the suitcase thing doesn't really work for me. I feel calmer if I imagine the worry as an ocean wave that I can float over. We learnt that in meditation at school as well.

'Wendy and I have some news,' Dad is saying. He takes hold of Wendy's hand.

'About the baby?'

'You know if it's a boy or a girl?'

'You've thought of a name?'

'You're moving home to Melbourne?' I ask.

'We're having twins!'

So that's why her tummy looks so big. I wonder if Mum knows.

Harry stops hoovering his sticky rice and looks up. His fringe is long, hangs over his eyes. His eyelashes are long, too, they always have been. 'Shit. Twins.'

This is quite a reaction for him. Harry used to react to everything. He used to get excited, but now I reckon if I told him a herd of elephants was at the front door he'd do his best to look bored.

'Chinese broccoli with oyster sauce? Rice noodle rolls?'

'Yes, yes,' says Jo. 'Two of the rice noodle rolls, thanks.' The waitress takes a pen from her pocket and scribbles on the card on our table.

'And can we see the drinks menu, please.' She turns to Dad. 'I think this calls for champagne!'

'Do you know whether they're boys or girls?' I ask Dad.

'We do, but we're not saying.'

'Oh, come on, tell us!' Jo almost shouts.

But they won't.

'It might be one of each,' I say.

The champagne arrives and Wendy doesn't have any but Dad and Jo do, and Jo proposes a toast to the twins. I don't feel like eating, or talking. Would the police have come to our house by now, spoken to Mum? But Wendy, sitting beside me, is looking at me so sweetly, I know she wants us to be friends, so I smile and imagine I've floated over a wave of worry and I pretend to be happy.

'Have you got twins in your family?' I ask her.

'None at all! Sometimes with IVF it can happen, it's more likely to happen.'

'It'll be an instant family!' says Jo.

'Dad already has a family,' says Harry. 'Had.'

'Oh, but you know what I mean, Harry darling!' She picks up the champagne glass that was put there for Wendy and turns to Dad. 'Can he have a bit of champagne?'

'Yes,' says Harry.

'No,' says Dad at the same time. 'Jo, he's only just seventeen.'

'All right, all right,' says Jo, 'keep your hair on.' She tops up her own glass. 'Better do what Dad says, hadn't we, Harry!'

'He wouldn't know what I'm allowed and not allowed to do.' Harry shrugs, and I want to punch him and say come on, please, I know it's hard but just try.

I think about what Jo said about an instant family. Right now, I'm the youngest of Dad's children. But I won't be anymore. I'll be someone in the middle. And I'm the only girl, Harry the only boy. We both have our places.

'They're IVF, like me,' I say out loud.

Silence. Maybe Wendy doesn't know?

I turn to Wendy. 'I was IVF too,' I explain.

Wendy nods, smiles at me, but it's an odd smile.

'Kind of like you, Lissa darling, yes,' says Jo quickly, patting my knee. 'So many different ways to have a baby now, aren't there! Now, where's that trolley with the roast duck? Anyone for more roast duck?'

'Yes, let's get another one,' says Dad, and he even picks out a plate of beef tripe.

'Yuck,' says Harry. 'I'm not eating that.'

'You don't have to,' says Dad, 'all the more for us.'

Jo pops some roast duck into her mouth. 'Have you chosen names?' Without waiting for an answer, she goes on. 'Androgynous names are the popular ones these days. Harriet – Harry, Charlotte – Charlie, Francesca – Frankie. And . . . Ashley, Cameron, Lindsey, they're all girls' names now.' Sometimes I think Dad asks Jo on these outings so there won't be any awkward silences with him, Wendy, me and Harry. Jo fills all the gaps.

'I've got a theory about it, actually,' Jo continues. We all sigh and roll our eyes and laugh a bit because Jo has many, many theories. 'People want their girls to grow up strong, so they give them a name that isn't too feminine. One that could also be a boy's name.'

'Do boys ever get names that were girls' names first?' I ask. 'Like, does it work the other way around?'

Jo shakes her head. 'I can't think of one example!'

Harry has stopped eating, he's looking at Jo and I hope he's not going to make fun of her opinions. Jo tops up her champagne. 'Just a theory of mine.'

I smile. 'Hey, remember when I was little how I wanted to be called Bruce? That was never an androgynous name! And Harry wanted to be called Gary?'

'You were such a funny little thing!' laughs Jo. 'I remember some days I had to call you Bruce and Harry Gary all day! Neither of you would answer to any other name. It did get a little tiresome I have to say. The Bruce and Gary game.' She shakes her head at me. 'You were obsessed with Bruce Springsteen! All the other kids loved Hi-5, or The Wiggles, but you'd be listening to "Born to Run", "Dancing in the Dark", all the hits. "Thunder Road". And even the lesser-known tracks! "Rosalita". "Growin' Up". Quite the little aficionado. What was it about you and Bruce Springsteen?' She downs her champagne, picks up a dumpling with her chopsticks and puts the whole thing into her mouth. 'I remember you once asked me if he was your dad,' Jo says with her mouth full of dumpling. 'You had some funny ideas. I wish I'd written them down.' She pours more champagne, turns to Harry, sitting on her other side. 'And you, you great big man, I don't know where you got the Gary from. Do you?'

'No.'

'Custard tart? Jelly?'

Jo takes two plates of square jelly in neat coloured stripes. The waitress doesn't look happy that Jo took them off the trolley herself, but Jo doesn't notice.

'Because it rhymed with Harry?' I suggest.

Harry shrugs.

'And remember when you first learnt to read, all you wanted to read was the dictionary! We bought you a kids' dictionary but you only wanted the great big one on the bookshelf. You wanted to read the whole thing by the time you turned eight.'

'Yeah, I remember. I never got past halfway through C, I don't think.' Reading words on their own like that is quite intense. I liked it though. I still play a game with myself where I open the dictionary at a random page and point to a word. That's how I've discovered some of my favourites. Like saudade. *The love that remains after someone or something has gone. The presence of absence.* Saudade. I like the soft 'd' sounds.

Jo is nudging Harry in that playful way she does, trying to get him to loosen up. 'How's football going? Been drafted by the mighty Cats yet?'

'Not yet,' says Harry, poking at his jelly with a fork.

'When's your next big match?'

Harry's eyes dart around. 'I've decided not to play the rest of this season.'

'We can talk about it later,' Dad says.

Harry narrows his eyes at Dad as if he's daring him to say something more.

'Just don't want you to waste your talent, mate.'

No one wants to upset the happy families and Dad moves the conversation on.

Jo says quietly to me, 'Quite the surly teenager these days, isn't he, darling?'

'Mango pudding. Taro dumpling. Turnip cake.'

'Yes, please,' says Wendy.

We finish with more Chinese tea and fortune cookies.

'I'll pick first,' says Jo, taking a cookie from the plate.

She makes a big deal of opening it up.

'You will be blinded by passion.'

'Well,' she says, blushing a bit, 'aren't I the lucky one! Open yours now, Harry darling.'

Harry crushes his cookie under his hand, but doesn't read the message or even look at it. Jo picks it up and reads it out.

'Your difficulties will strengthen you. That's good advice, darling. Remember that. You keep that one, Harry.'

'My turn,' says Wendy, and she opens hers.

'Happy life is in front of you.'

Dad smiles. 'I already have a happy life,' she says, and Dad kisses her on the cheek. Harry doesn't look impressed, but I think it's nice.

'My turn?' Dad opens his up.

'You have some new tricks up your sleeve.'

'I wonder?' says Jo. 'What new tricks, little brother?'

'I bet I know a trick you can do!' I say, remembering the science class. 'I bet you can roll your tongue.'

He tries, he looks ridiculous, but he can't do it, and even Harry smiles.

'Well then, how come I can do it?' I demonstrate it perfectly. 'Mum can't do it either. Can you, Jo?'

Jo tries but she's hopeless too.

'I need to tell our teacher. I can tell her we're a rare case!'

'Maybe you got swapped at birth,' says Harry. 'And you're not really my sister.'

It's like his one contribution to the whole lunchtime conversation.

'Thanks, Harry. I'm sorry but we actually look pretty alike.'

Now Wendy's trying. Yes! Wendy can do it!

'But I think that theory's been disproven in scientific studies,' says Wendy, pouring more tea into her little cup and then Dad's cup as well. 'You haven't opened your cookie, Lissa.'

I open it.

'A lifetime friend shall soon be made.'

I hope that comes true. I need a new lifetime friend.

'Let's take one home for Mum,' I say.

'And Troy,' says Harry.

Since when was Harry so keen on including Troy?

Dad pays the bill, and we go down to Federation Square where our cars are, and then Dad suggests a walk along the river. Harry doesn't want to, but Dad insists.

It's a beautiful afternoon. The winter sun is shining and everything looks soft and sharp at the same time. It's cold but if you walk in the sun there's a gentle warmth in it.

I need to get Dad on his own so I can ask him if he knows anything about Reed. He's walking with Wendy, holding hands, and Jo and I are behind them. It's good to be moving, walking all that food off. Jo and Wendy start talking about business because Wendy's an architect and Jo's always got some project going on with her colour forecasting. She has a theory that people are afraid of colour. Wendy doesn't design houses, she works on big projects like airports and public buildings. Jo has such a loud voice. 'Minimalism! I'm so over it!' she almost shouts. 'Get some bold colour, get some pattern into your interiors, people!'

Harry's walking on his own, head down, up ahead.

I move over to Dad.

'Dad, I need to ask you something.'

'Sure, what is it, Liss?' He puts his arm around me and looks out over the river as we walk along.

'Do you know someone called Reed Lister?'

'No.'

'You've never heard of anyone called that name?'

Dad shakes his head. 'Who is he?'

'He's someone who's made contact with Mum, I think.'

'How old is he?'

160

'Thirteen.'

'Oh.' Dad seems relieved. 'I thought you meant he was older.'

'No.'

'Well, I don't know anyone called Reed, Liss.'

'Mum might have, um, known him when he was a baby. Like, do you know anything about a baby thirteen years ago?'

'Only you, darling.' He smiles. 'Still with your funny questions, your crazy words.' He squeezes me close as we walk along.

After our walk when we're back at the car, we say goodbye to Jo. She's got a sportscar, I don't know what type it is but Harry's pretty impressed.

'I've been doing some driving,' he says, looking at Dad. 'Troy took me.'

All of a sudden, Harry loves Troy.

Seeing Dad again has made me feel weird about Troy, but when we get home, guess who's there, helping Mum put up a trellis for the apple tree.

'We need to clean up the shed,' says Mum. 'It's a real mess.' Harry looks a bit alarmed and I think he's worried they've found his alcohol stash. I'm relieved that no one is mentioning a visit from the police. Or Lorraine.

'I got you a fortune cookie,' I say to Mum. 'And Harry got one for you, Troy.'

Troy looks really happy and so does Mum.

'Come on,' I say, 'open them up.'

'In the end all things will be known. Well, that's cryptic.' Mum screws up the piece of paper and puts it in the bin. 'What does yours say, Troy?'

'Your success will astonish everyone.'

'Wow, go Troy,' I say, and he doesn't screw his up.

Troy leaves, it's after 2 pm but neither Harry nor I want lunch because we're so full from the yum cha brunch. Mum makes a toastie for herself and she's sitting at the kitchen bench looking at her phone.

I go into Harry's room. He's on his computer.

I sit on his bed. 'Wow, twins,' I say. 'What do you reckon about that?'

He ignores me.

Silence. The computer clicks.

I have to ask him, because I really don't get what's happening. 'Okay,' I say, 'it's no big deal but I just want to know so I can understand –'

'I don't care if they're having twins,' Harry says angrily. 'I couldn't care less.'

'I wasn't talking about that. I want to know why you told me you deleted that nude as soon as you got it. When you only deleted it like two days ago?'

He keeps playing his game. 'Don't know.'

'Harry, I'm trying to help you!' He's so frustrating!

He pauses the game but won't look at me.

'I don't know why I didn't delete it at first!' he bursts out. 'No one had ever sent me a nude . . . I was . . . look, I don't know why, okay!' He runs his fingers through his hair. 'But, Liss, I never sent it to anyone, never showed anyone or told anyone. And it's gone now, you can check.'

'Don't worry, I don't need to check.'

'So you reckon it must be the footy guys who made that profile?' I ask.

He nods. 'I bet they got the pic off my phone. They've set me up, I reckon.'

'And set Amber up,' I add. 'She's so mad at you, she thinks you did this.'

He puts his head in his hands. 'Why didn't I delete it when I first got it?'

Just like Reed, Harry's asking questions I can't answer.

He looks up, stares out the window. 'Some of the guys are awful to her.'

'To Amber? Like, how?'

'Making jokes behind her back. She tries to flirt with them, she says she's older than she is, it's pretty tragic. Some of them pretend they're interested in her, she makes such a fool of herself.'

'She seems really confident at school.'

Harry's doodling on a post-it note on his desk. Angry scribbles and arrows fill the little page. 'These guys are older, like three years older than her. They're not interested in her, except as a kind of . . .' Harry grimaces, '. . . sport.' Then suddenly he looks right at me and says, 'You need to be careful when you start going out with guys, Liss. The way some guys talk about girls, how they rate them, how they have these competitions to see who can make out with the most girls over a footy season. They're always getting girls to send them nudes and stuff like that, then they show them around, sometimes they sell them. It's really off.'

I wonder which guys. 'Like Robbo?'

'Robbo has this tally sheet . . . And they think it's so funny to airdrop like, really gross pictures, to random girls on the train and then wait for their reaction.'

'You can say it, Harry. I know what they are.'

He looks up from his arrows. 'They haven't sent you one, have they? They haven't airdropped –'

'Don't worry! They've never sent me anything.'

'You need to keep your settings on private.' He jumps up. 'Where's your phone? Who knows what they're going to do now.' He's starting to panic. 'Jesus, I don't want them to go after you as well.'

I follow Harry out to the living room, where my phone is charging on the bench.

Mum's finishing her toastie, still scrolling. 'What's the problem with the phone?'

'No problem.' Harry's checking the profiles, he doesn't look up.

'No?' Mum can tell something's going on.

'Liss?'

I try to sound casual. 'Yeah?'

'I've just got a text from Amber's mother.' Mum slides her phone across the bench to us. It's one line.

Expect a call from the police

'No,' says Harry.

Silence. Mum stares at Harry and then at me. 'Do either of you know what she's talking about?'

Harry can't look at Mum.

'Mum, she's a drama queen,' I say, but Harry is speaking too.

'There's all this shit on social media,' he says quietly.

'What?'

I want to tell Harry that the police aren't after him, Lorraine's talking about Reed! She will have called the police about Reed, not Harry. She mightn't know anything about that Rate Year Eight post!

'Is this cyber bullying?' Mum's trying, but even the way she says those two words makes it clear that she has no idea what it means.

'Whatever you want to call it,' Harry mutters.

'Why are the police involved? Harry?'

He doesn't even speak. Just stands looking outside.

'Mum,' I say, 'you know what Lorraine's like. She lives her life like it's some reality TV show.'

'True, but why is she sending me this text?' Mum is baffled. 'Unless it was meant for someone else? You don't even use social media, do you? Harry?'

'Nup,' says Harry. He wipes tears from his eyes, doesn't want us to see.

'What on earth is going on?' Mum looks at me now.

'People have . . . spread rumours,' I say. 'That Harry's, like, disrespectful to girls. It's just total rumours, Mum, Harry hasn't done anything.' I think of that photo in his phone.

'How ridiculous. We should report it to the school. It's against the law.'

'Wouldn't help.' Harry turns around. He's composed himself. 'Nobody cares.'

Mum's being all adult and logical. 'Look, I know Lorraine can exaggerate, can tend to blow things out of proportion.

I really don't think the police would be interested in some silly rumours. I might just give her a call –'

'No!' shouts Harry. Then, 'Please, Mum, don't call her. If the police call you then I'll talk to them.'

'I honestly can't believe that will happen!' says Mum. 'If you've done nothing wrong? I'm sure Lorraine's overreacting, you're right, she may not have even spoken with the police.' Mum shakes her head. 'I mean, this is ridiculous. How long has this been going on for? These rumours about you?'

'A while.'

'Why didn't you tell me? Or Dad?'

Harry shrugs.

'Is Amber involved?'

Harry doesn't react. I nod.

'When something's done against you, you can talk to people, Harry, get it sorted out. Young people should tell an adult. We've always taught you that. And if it's necessary then adults can involve the legal system.'

'Mum, people your age don't get it, that's not the way the world works.' Harry sighs like an old man. 'Kids get destroyed on social media all the time.'

'Didn't some expert come to the school to talk about cyber safety?' Mum asks. 'I remember signing the form. Digital health or something?'

'Yeah, maybe, whatever.'

'What did they say about respectful communication?'

'What do you mean?' says Harry.

'I *mean*,' says Mum forcefully, 'when people speak politely to each other. With respect. Treat each other as human beings. Show dignity.'

Harry snorts. 'I don't think so.'

'What, so people can say whatever they like? To the entire world? Regardless of the facts? Is that what these people are doing to you?'

'Pretty much. And it's not only kids who do this, Mum. It's heaps of people. Even the media. You can't believe anything or anyone these days.'

'That's lawless. No respect for the rules, for any authority. For the truth!' Mum's getting all outraged on his behalf. I feel sick because I'm the one who's involved the police, not Harry. It's me and Reed!

'There are no rules,' says Harry. 'The truth is too complicated.' He sits down at the bench. 'And in case you hadn't noticed, dear Mother, authority has kind of let us down.'

'That's very cynical, Harry,' says Mum. 'Surely the law is the last bastion of authority that we respect.' Mum picks up her coffee cup, goes over to the dishwasher, glances at her phone again. 'Once there's no respect for laws, for basic fairness, justice, for honesty, where are we at?'

I look outside at the fading afternoon light.

'Here, I suppose,' says Harry.

The three of us sit there for a while. It's not just me this time. None of us knows what to say or do.

Then Mum says, 'Can you tell me more about these rumours? And who's behind them? I think I need a bit more information, Harry.'

But Harry gets up.

'Harry?'

'Don't make me talk about this now,' he says, and heads back to his room.

Mum sighs. 'Do you think I should contact the school?' she asks me. 'Would that be the best thing to do?'

'I don't know.'

Would Lorraine have given the police Mum's mobile number? Probably.

But the afternoon wears on and no police call us. Mum tries to call Lorraine but thank god she doesn't pick up. She actually never picks up. I'm waiting for a moment when I can go to Hana's and tell Reed that Dad knows nothing, that he has to go home before the police arrest him. Will he be charged with kidnapping? Will I?

I get my science homework and sit at the table staring at it.

'Liss, are you involved in this as well?'

'Not really.'

'I don't understand. Are Harry's friends sticking up for him?'

'People get scared that they'll be cancelled too.'

'Cancelled? Is that what you call it?'

'Yeah.'

Mum nods, trying to take it all in.

'Do these things eventually blow over?'

I think of Harry in his room. They might move on to someone else, but what happens to him now?

'I'll speak with your father about it,' Mum says, 'although he's got a lot on his plate right now.' She pauses.

'Yeah, did you know that they're having twins?'

Mum nods. 'Dad told me last week, yes.'

Just another thing she didn't tell me. She sits at the table, sighs a bit sadly. Maybe she's remembering when things were simpler. When we were a family, together. Years ago.

'Sorry, Liss, with all this going on I didn't even ask you earlier, did you and Harry have a nice time with your dad?'

'Yeah, we did.'

'And you're okay with the whole twins news?'

'Yep,' I say, although I don't really know how I feel about it.

Mum's face relaxes a bit. 'That's good.'

We keep sitting. I flip through the pages of my textbook.

'And we did the tongue test,' I tell Mum. 'Dad can't do it either. Or Jo. Mrs Tellier will be interested to know. Wendy could do it,' I add, 'so the twins might be able to as well. Imagine if one twin could do it and the other couldn't? That would be an interesting experim—'

'I wouldn't worry about that silly tongue test, Liss.'

Then I remember that odd moment with Jo and Wendy at the table. 'It was weird, when we were talking about the twins, Jo said their IVF is different from the IVF you had with me. I don't get how it would be different. Is that because it's in China?'

'It's not different.'

'Did they have IVF because of Dad's cancer? Like you did with me? Mum?'

'I presume so. Once someone's had cancer treatment, often the only way they can have a baby is using IVF.' She looks at me. 'You know all about that, Liss. How you're IVF because

Dad had been treated for cancer.' She glances towards Harry's room. 'Now's not the time to go over it again.'

I do know all about this. I've always known, I don't really remember being told for the first time, I think it was when I was in prep. Heaps of people are IVF. It's never been a big deal.

'And the twins.'

'Yes.'

'Except Jo said it was only *kind of* like me. And Wendy had this funny look on her face.' I glance down at the book. Diagrams, genes, recessive and dominant . . . 'I just wonder what she meant. That mine was different.'

I'm almost putting it down to Jo talking crap and exaggerating half the time, and maybe the champagne as well. And sometimes I hear words differently, read too much into words because I think about them so much . . . But there's the email, Mum's not telling me something, and I wonder if this is part of it . . .

'Maybe it was nothing, Mum – but, like, thirteen years ago, and Reed Lister, the email, I know you got his email –'

Mum stands up.

'Liss . . .' She stops me, takes my hand.

'Yes?'

Leads me over to the couch.

'What?' I say. Mum looks very pale. 'What's wrong?'

'Come over here, darling, sit down.'

Her hand is shaking in mine.

'We should have told you this a long time ago . . .'

'It's like when they fight, they're fighting inside me.'

'You're all they talk about. They, like, live for you.'

13

ALONE

A Lone. Solo. Lonely. Alone.

So many ls and os.

Wow.

You think you know people but you don't. Even your parents.

'Liss, I'm so sorry we didn't tell you this before.'

'Tell me what?'

And I think she's going to finally explain about that email, and Reed . . .

'Remember we've told you how Dad was sick before you were born?'

'Yeah.'

'He had a lot of chemotherapy.'

'I know, you've told me all this.'

'We had Harry before Dad got sick. Then he got sick and it was terrible. Then when he got better, we wanted another child so much, but there was no guarantee that Dad would ever be able to have another one. The doctors said it might take one to four years for his sperm to go back to normal after the treatment, they said with some people it takes up to ten years, or it might never go back to normal.'

I nod.

'Well, we tried for three years, with no luck. The doctors had frozen some of Dad's sperm, but it wasn't working. I was getting older and all the IVF cycles were exhausting us.'

I keep nodding.

'The medical advice was –'

'What?' I ask.

'Well . . . so we used a donor, a sperm donor.'

My breathing stops.

'Lissa, darling, you were totally born from love.'

'Oh.'

Slowly, like a wave about to crash, that I can't float over, it comes to me.

I am not my father's daughter.

Everything starts to slip away, everything I thought I knew, the way the world was. It wasn't. Isn't.

My dad is not my biological father.

Harry is only my half-brother.

Jo is not my aunty.

What?

What?

'What about the twins?'

Mum's eyes are glistening. 'It turns out after ten years, Dad's sperm did go back to normal. They still needed IVF but they could use his sperm and Wendy's eggs. So that's how it's different from your IVF, darling.'

Harry, the twins, they're all Dad's children. But not me. 'So the twins, they won't be any relation to me at all.'

'Liss, don't think about it like that, it's not like that.'

'Why didn't Dad tell me? Why didn't you tell me?'

'We told you that you were IVF. We felt that was enough for then, and then we were always waiting for the right time to explain . . .'

'What other secrets have you kept from me?'

'None.'

'What about Reed? What about the three pregnancies?' I shout.

'What?'

'Don't lie to me!'

'Liss, darling, we were trying to protect you.'

'I don't feel protected!' I yell. 'I feel very unprotected. So it didn't work!'

I get up. I don't know where I'm going. You know that saying about the rug being pulled out from under you? I'm tripping, stumbling, every step feels like that second before you fall over. I want to run, run away like Reed, and never come back.

The hallway's on an angle, like I'm on a ship.

Whose daughter am I?

I run to the front door.

'Liss, come back!'

Someone has put a business card under our door.

Victoria Police
Please call us as soon as possible.

I open the door.

'What are you doing here?'

Reed is standing there, out of breath.

'It's Mercy, she's in trouble. I don't think she's breathing.'

Like you crashed your car because you were texting.
Or left a candle burning and your whole house burnt down.
Or had a baby when you weren't old enough.
Or kept a secret that would change everything.
I wonder if that's what happens to some people?
That they make a mistake they can't come back from.

14

SURRENDER

I slam the door and start running.

'We have to go to the hospital,' I tell Reed.

'Should we call an uber?'

'I don't have my phone, I don't have any money and I don't have an uber account.' I'm still running, wildly running down the road. Away from my mother and the life that wasn't mine.

Reed catches up with me. Mercy is limp in his arms. Oh god.

'An ambulance?'

'It'll be quicker to run. It's close, five minutes, past the railway line, before Chemist Warehouse.'

'She won't drink from the bottle.'

She's still in the sling, he's tried to do it properly but it's a total fail, he's holding her against him as he runs.

'Is she breathing?'

'We can't stop!' He shouts at me, scared. 'We have to get there!'

We're running together. 'She was crying and crying and

then,' he puffs, 'she ran out of energy and whimpered and then that stopped too.'

Reed is sweating. 'I tried,' takes a breath, 'to look after her.'

'You're only a kid, you're thirteen.' I'm shouting now too. 'You can't do this.'

But he can't not do it, either. Both those things are pretty obvious to us now.

It's hard to run holding a baby, and Reed does this rapid shuffle. We get there in record time. I'm a hopeless runner, but I think we've both got a bit of that hysterical strength right now.

There's the sign. Emergency.

The entrance. Glass doors slide open.

A window. Admission here.

We stop, we're both puffing and sweating and Mercy seems still. I want so much to hear her funny snoring. Even her screaming would be good, now.

Her skin is cold. She looks terrible. Her hair is all sweaty and stuck to her head. She is breathing, I think, but there's a long time between breaths. They're raspy.

A bored-looking woman with glasses a bit like Reed's looks up at us.

'Name?'

'She's not breathing properly,' Reed pants.

The woman stands up, leans forward to look through the glass at us, at Mercy.

She calls for someone. An alarm sounds.

'Code blue to emergency. Code blue.'

People are running. A guy in green scrubs appears and lifts

Mercy from Reed's arms. He rushes back behind the admitting area. Reed starts to follow him.

'Stay here,' the woman in glasses orders him. 'You need to admit the patient, then you can go with it.'

'Her,' says Reed.

She hands us a clipboard with a pen attached. 'Fill out this form.'

She's not very polite. How about please and thank you?

Surname.

'Is it Lister?' Reed asks me. It's one of those questions.

'It'll do for now.' My heart is racing. I try to focus on what's happening, on the form. Who knows what any of our surnames should be. Mine, Reed's. Mercy's.

Given names.

Mercy. 'I don't know if she's got a second name.'

'Just leave it blank.'

Your name.

Reed Lister.

Relationship to the patient.

Uncle.

We get stuck on the next question.

Are you admitting as a public or private patient?

Reed leans in towards the glass. 'Excuse me?'

The woman is looking at her computer screen, totally ignores him.

'Um, this question here?' Reed is holding up the sheet, pointing with the pen. His fingernails are dirty.

'Yes?' she says as if we're the most annoying thing that's ever happened to her.

'I don't know if I write public or private patient.'

'Doesn't matter.'

'Sorry?'

'Doesn't matter. If it's emergency then it's public.'

'So do I write public?'

She's back on her screen, doesn't answer again.

'Just write public,' I say, and I glare at the woman because she is SO rude and can't she tell that Reed and I are freaking out here?

Next question: Medicare details.

'I don't know them either!' Reed whispers frantically, pushes his glasses back up his nose, and we're both too scared to ask again so we leave it blank.

Next of kin.

'Me again?' Reed asks.

I nod.

Current medications and dosage.

Reed writes None.

Allergies.

None.

Patient's GP.

We leave that blank as well.

Reed hands the sheet back to her under the glass.

The woman takes it, reads it.

'Can we go with her now?' he asks.

'You need to fill out the GP details.'

She scans the rest of the document.

Then she looks over the top of her glasses at him. Her mouth turns down at the edges. 'How old are you?'

'Thirteen.'

'Do you have any ID?'

Reed shakes his head. 'Can we see Mercy now? I need to go with her.'

She looks more closely at Reed. His hair is still neat because it's so short, but he hasn't had a shower in all this time. His clothes are dirty. His hands are dirty, too.

'Wait there.'

She's talking to another nurse, who picks up a phone. She goes and speaks to someone else. Maybe they think we're too young.

Oh god, I have a bad feeling that something has happened to Mercy.

We sit and wait. Another woman comes up and says, 'Someone will be with you shortly.'

Who? When?

Thoughts, a wave, a suitcase. Nothing is ever going to be okay.

We keep sitting. Reed gets out his hanky and cleans his glasses. It reminds me of my grandpa. Hang on, he's not my grandpa.

I take deep breaths. I don't want to think about what my mother told me. I don't want to think about Harry. I just want Mercy to be okay.

I reach into the pocket of my North Face to check my phone, then remember I don't have it. All I can do is look at what is happening around me. Not think. A clock. Quarter to five. There's a woman with a baby and a little kid. I hear an ambulance somewhere. A girl on crutches in her netball outfit. She's a Goal Attack. A man who keeps asking where he can have a cigarette. 'You must be two hundred metres from the doors,' says the woman with the glasses. An old lady arrives in a wheelchair being pushed by a guy with tattoos of bears on his arms. A light flickers somewhere, like the globe needs replacing.

We keep waiting. What's happening? Where's Mercy?

'I know you think it was stupid,' says Reed suddenly, 'to take Mercy. But I had no choice.'

I nod. I can't have this conversation. Any conversation.

'The first time I went after she was born, she was lying on their mattress on the floor. There are rats in that house, I've seen them.'

I'm not sure what to say to that. I can't focus on what he's saying. I can't even see straight. I'm seeing like in a dream, or a painting that is moving, blocks of colour and shape, not real at all.

'We had an excursion to Melbourne, to the gallery. I forged a note from Mum saying that I could get a later train home. Mercy was two weeks old.'

'So, like, really small,' I say, pointlessly.

'They don't even have a heater at that house, they just break up their back fence and burn it in the fireplace.'

'Oh . . .'

'At the gallery, they had these paintings from kids, it was called the Young Archies. We all had to enter it, paint a portrait. Heaps of us painted our parents. I painted Dad, using photos. I knew it wouldn't be selected because I'm no good at Art, and also it was hard to get his hands right.'

Why is he raving on about this now? And that word. Dad. It sounds odd to me. Dad. My dad.

'I painted my father with these kind of melting hands, like his hands were falling away from him.' Reed spreads out his own hands, his fingers, studies them. 'I can't draw hands very well.'

Two police come in. A man and a woman. I'm wondering if they might have come with the ambulance.

They don't go to the counter.

They come towards us.

Oh no.

Dark blue, pale blue, black shoes. A badge.

'Reed Lister?' the policewoman says.

Reed doesn't stand up, look her in the eye, shake her hand. He peers up at them, frightened.

'You'll need to come with us.'

'Come on, Reed,' says the policeman, 'stand up.'

'I can't leave Mercy,' Reed tries to explain. 'I need to stay with Mercy. I'm responsible for –'

'The doctors will look after Mercy.'

'I promised Eliot! My brother. I'm her uncle. I'm next of kin.' He's panicking. 'It says on the form.'

'Stand up,' says the policeman again.

'It's okay, Reed,' I tell him, 'I can wait here, for Mercy.' He doesn't hear me because his voice is loud and high and he's telling them he can't leave her.

'Calm down, mate, we're just going to another room.' The policeman puts a hand firmly on Reed's shoulder and guides him towards the back of the emergency department.

'Don't take me away from her, please! I need to check on her, need to know that she's okay!' It's the first time I've seen

Reed start to lose it. He's ducking down, trying to shake the policeman's arm off, but the policeman has a firm grip on him. Is Reed going to make a run for it?

The nurse ushers Reed and the police officers in behind the counter. I get up and follow them. I'm coming. He needs me.

The police don't stop me. We go past a whiteboard with lots of names and illnesses and injuries written beside them. The netball girl must be: ankle break? The little kid could be: measles? Next to another name is: broken hip. Mercy Lister: nothing next to her name. Is that a good or bad sign? It's the sort of question Reed would ask me. I can't see Mercy anywhere. We follow the fast-walking nurse down a corridor of cubicles separated by curtains. Each cubicle has a number at the top, where the curtain is on a rod. Machines beep but the nurses and doctors seem to ignore them. I see the netball girl sitting on a trolley. I see the smoking man pacing in one cubicle, looking agitated.

We get to a room with a sign on the door. Quiet Room. The policeman opens the door and we go in. There's a low table and some chairs, a painting of a beach, nothing else.

'Sit down,' says the policeman. 'Can we get your name?'

'Lissa, that's L-I-S-S-A, Freeman.'

'Phone number for Mum or Dad?'

I give them Mum's mobile.

'I'll give her a call,' says the policewoman and she starts to head out.

I want to say so many things. Like, please tell her that I'm okay, I'm sorry I ran off like that, I can explain all this with

Reed, I didn't want to keep these secrets, why didn't you tell me you'd received his email? Why didn't you tell me –

'Do you need mine, too?' Reed asks.

'We already called your parents. They're on their way, should be here soon.' The policeman stands up. 'You two wait here, I'll get the paperwork.'

'Can you find out if Mercy's okay? My . . .' he pauses as if he's about to ask me what she is, but answers the question himself. 'My niece?'

'I'll see what I can do.' The officer closes the door. I hear a click.

We sit there. Reed's looking down at his hands again – small and grimy, open in his lap – as if they hold some answer to the mess we're in.

He turns to me, his green eyes wide and frightened. 'Do you think Mercy will be okay?'

What I'm actually thinking is that her breathing was really shallow. And I'm worried about that rash. Her cough, too. And I'm thinking of everything I googled about not giving babies cow's milk, not water, not even bottled water . . .

But I touch Reed on the arm and say, 'Yeah, I think so.'

More minutes pass. I wish they'd come and tell us what's happening.

'My parents are coming,' Reed moans, his head in his hands. 'Have we broken the law? Have I?' Before I can try to answer that question, Reed bursts out, 'Why did I tell them my real name? I'm such an idiot!'

'We would have got caught anyway. The police had already come to my place and left their card. I saw it when I was walking out of the house.'

'Were you coming to find me at Hana's place?'

'I don't know where I was going. I was just, I don't know, getting out.'

Reed nods.

It's very quiet in the Quiet Room.

Reed picks up a magazine. A bushfire on the cover. The headline reads 'One hundred species on the brink of extinction'.

Something feels as if it's unravelling, like one of Jo's big stripy knitted blankets. Something solid slipping away, disappearing row by row.

'Reed?'

He looks up at me.

'I'm not who I thought I was either.'

Before I can explain, the police are back. 'Mercy's with the doctors now. They'll take her up to ICU. She's in good hands.'

Thank god.

'So she's breathing?' Reed asks.

'Yes, son, she's breathing.'

'What's ICU?'

'Intensive care unit. Now it's our turn for some questions, okay?'

They tell us their names – Roger and Faye. They ask Reed lots of questions, about where he's been and about how he's spent the last five days.

Intensive care unit. Isn't that where people go when they're really sick and might die?

After about twenty minutes, there's a knock at the door. Reed startles, like it can only be bad news.

It's the nurse, with Reed's parents. 'Reed, Reed, oh, Reed, thank god.' Reed's mother rushes to him, hugging him against her. I recognise them from the photo I googled. Reed's mother looks older than my mum, shorter and heavier. Her hair is short and grey, and she's wearing a dark blue cardigan, all done up with little buttons. 'Thank god you're all right. We were so worried.'

'Thank you for locating him,' says the tall man who must be Reed's dad. He has short hair like Reed. He stands up straight, puts a hand on Reed's shoulder. He's wearing a green tie. 'Reed, son . . .' His voice cracks. 'Please, never.'

Reed's mum pulls back from him. 'Look at you, you're filthy, where have you been? You're not hurt?'

'Not hurt,' says Reed, standing with his arms straight, his hands by his sides as they hug him.

'Now, we need some paperwork from you both, and then we can release Reed into your custody. You may need to make another statement at your local police station. From Ballarat, are you? Peter, and,' he glances down at his notes, 'Jan?'

Reed's father nods.

'What about his, er, sorry, who are you?' asks Reed's mother.

'Lissa,' says Reed.

'Her mother's on her way,' says Roger, the policeman. Then he gives a bit of a speech. 'You've caused quite a lot of trouble for your parents here, and the police. We hope you've learnt your lesson, Reed. Both of you.' He turns to the parents. 'I'm glad we've found him. It doesn't always end up with the happy family reunion.'

Reed's parents keep thanking the police. At this stage it doesn't look as if we're going to get in a heap of trouble.

The policewoman asks Reed's mum and dad some questions about Mercy.

'We're so sorry to cause you inconvenience,' Reed's dad says. 'It's a family matter.'

'The infant is about to be moved up to ICU,' says the policewoman. 'I'm sure they're doing all they can for her.'

'Can we see her now?' Reed asks.

The policeman takes us out again and we walk in single file past the trolleys and beds, past the Goal Attack and the old woman in the wheelchair, and then we turn right, down another corridor to a place with more curtained-off beds. Mercy's in a clear plastic crib on a trolley. Reed rushes over. She's not wearing the onesie we bought her, her little arms and neck are all we can see under a white cotton blanket. I think she's asleep. A nurse has taped something onto Mercy's arm. 'IV antibiotics,' she says. There's some other drip on her arm that's connected to a bag of clear liquid on a trolley. She has a clear plastic mask over her face. She seems to be attached to a monitor with cords. She doesn't even really look like Mercy, we can hardly see her.

'Will Mercy be okay?' Reed asks me, the nurse, anyone.

'This will help,' says the nurse, which doesn't really answer the question.

'Sorry, Mercy, I'm so sorry,' he whispers and only I can hear him.

Reed stands beside her crib like she's his project at a school presentation. He holds one arm out towards the crib. 'This is Mercy,' he says to his parents. 'Eliot's baby.' His voice starts to tremble. 'He had a baby . . .' and then Reed stands there, arms by his sides, and he's crying, sobbing, his shoulders shaking like suddenly he's let it all go, this looking after a baby, this needing to find out who he was, and his tears drop, fall off his face and land on his hoodie, even the floor. He takes off his glasses, rubs the tears from his eyes but they keep falling. His face gets dirtier because his hands are so dirty and now the tears are making the dirt smear everywhere. He looks so young when he doesn't have his glasses on. Reed goes to his mum and then everyone in the room is crying. Everyone except Mercy.

'We know,' says Reed's mum. 'We found him, he told us.'

They move Mercy out of the cubicle in Emergency and we all go in a lift to ICU on the third floor – Mercy in her little trolley crib on wheels. She's attached by a tube to a different trolley that has a machine on it that's beeping, and the bag of clear liquid hanging down.

Mercy gets a whole room to herself. And her own nurse to look after her.

We have to wash and sterilise our hands. We all stand there, outside Mercy's room while they organise her special crib and things. I wonder if my mum will know where to come when she gets to the hospital? That mean lady downstairs mightn't tell her. I also feel like I should leave because Reed and his parents will have things to talk about.

A woman comes in. She's younger than my mum, she wears a lanyard with Kristina written on it, I can't read her surname. She's carrying a folder, she has long slim fingers. 'I'm Dr Edstrom,' she says. 'If you'd like to follow me, we can give you some information about Mercy now.' We follow her out into an alcove next to Mercy's room where there are some chairs lined up. We move them into a little semicircle. There's a big window and it's dark outside. Specks of sparkling rain hit the glass.

The doctor sits down too. 'Mercy's malnourished, she has mild hypothermia, she's dehydrated, and we're checking her for whooping cough.'

'Yes, she has a bad cough,' says Reed, trying to give some helpful feedback.

'Will she be okay, Doctor –'

'Call me Kristina. It's lucky you got her here when you did. The next twenty-four hours will be crucial. Has Mercy been immunised?'

'I wouldn't have thought so,' says Reed's mother.

'Do you know anything about the circumstances of her birth? Was it a straightforward labour?'

'I'm sorry, we don't know any of those details.'

'Can we stay here, with her? I need to stay with her,' says Reed.

'In ICU we can admit two or three visitors at a time, so take it in turns going in, but you can stay as long as you like.'

'Thanks, thanks, Kristina,' says Reed, trying to be an adult. 'I'm next of kin.'

Kristina smiles at Reed, smooths down her shiny long hair.

'Just wait in this area while they get her organised. The nurse will let you know when you can go in.'

We sit in our little semicircle of chairs like friends at a party.

No one asks Reed a question, but he suddenly bursts out with an answer. 'I was angry, I wanted to find my mother!'

'Reed, I am your mother.'

Reed's dad is sitting straight and still. 'We always intended to tell you, when you were ready.'

'I mean my biological mother. And I had that email, from her. I was only trying to find her . . .'

As if by magic, that is the moment my mother arrives.

She's been running. 'Liss,' she pants, 'what's going on?'

There's an awkward meeting between Reed's parents and Mum. They shake hands, pull another chair into the circle.

'Our son ran away and it appears he's, ah, teamed up with your daughter.'

Mum turns to Reed. 'Your son?'

'It's Reed,' I tell Mum. 'Reed Lister.'

She looks so shocked, like she might faint. She sits down. 'Oh god,' she says, losing her breath again, her hand on her chest. 'What? What's happened?'

'Don't worry, Mum, nobody's hurt or anything.'

'I sent you an email,' says Reed.

Mum is staring at him, shaking her head.

'The email?' He continues. 'I think you're my mother.'

Mum shakes her head more, but she's crying. What does she know?

He leans closer to her, opens his hands. 'I really believe you might be.'

'Reed, listen,' sobs Reed's mum. 'This lady can't be your mother.'

'Why not?' demands Reed, turning to face her. 'Why can't she?'

'Because your biological mother is no longer alive.'

Reed stands up, stumbles.

His father stands too and moves closer to him. 'Steady, son.'

Reed looks so sad, so confused. 'Dead?'

'She never met you,' says Reed's mother, gently.

'How could my own mother never have met me? That can't be true.'

Reed's dad steps forward and all Reed's formal little ways make sense. He's learnt them from this man. 'We planned to tell you when you were an adult, when your life was on the right track.'

'How did she die?' Reed shouts at them. 'If she never met me?'

'She . . . we believe it was suicide. How could we have told you that?' Reed's mum starts to sob again, sits down, her head in her hands.

But my mum is saying something and she's getting louder. 'No, no, no, no.'

Everyone else stops and looks at her.

'That's not what happened.'

Reed's father frowns. 'I'm sorry? How do you know?'

'Because I was there.'

Those banners, I'd seen them often. Bedsheets sewn together, red writing painted across them, tied onto the fencing of the overpass.

This time there were no sheets, they only had spray cans.

She had to write upside down . . .

15

SAUDADE

We all turn to Mum.

What?

'I'm so sorry, I don't know how to talk about this. I've never . . .'

She beckons Reed over. He stands in front of her.

'Reed, it's so good to meet you.' She takes his hand, clutches it with both of hers like she never wants to let go. 'I've thought of you so often, over the years. I've hoped you had a loving family, that you were happy.'

Reed nods, and keeps nodding, like he's trying to make Mum feel better about everything that he doesn't understand by nodding.

'I did, I do,' he says.

Mum turns to the parents. 'I'm sorry,' she says, 'this is very difficult.'

Nobody says anything.

Mum starts to speak.

'Thirteen years ago . . . It was January, just before the long weekend. Liss, you were a baby, in your car-seat in the back, we were on the freeway. It was just after four, I think it was a Thursday. I was visiting a friend in Clifton Hill. She hadn't met you yet. Her name was Kath, my friend, we've lost contact now . . . The radio,' Mum says as if it's come back into her mind this moment. 'It was "Landslide", the Fleetwood Mac song.'

What a strange detail to tell us now.

'It was stormy, windy. Hot, but the weather was about to break. One side of the sky was dark grey and the other bright sunlight. I was coming up to an overpass – a footbridge, not a road – over the freeway.' She turns suddenly to Reed's parents. 'Did you ever see those banners? Save the Wombat State Forest. On the Eastern Freeway overpasses? People put them up, police took them down, people made more, and put them up, the police took them down. Did you see it?'

Reed's parents look blank, we all stare at my mother, who's looking past us now, like part of her is somewhere else, long ago. She's not making a lot of sense.

'Someone was standing on the footbridge, the sun was shining on her, the light was dramatic. Young. Her hair was flying all around her, she kept pushing it back from her face. She was leaning over the fencing. Did she have one leg over? Half on the wrong side . . .' Mum frowns, shakes her head. 'She was holding a spray can, she wrote a letter, the start of a letter on the concrete, her message, the forest, writing upside down . . . She wore a dress but I could see from the sun, from her silhouette, that she was pregnant. Her dress was flimsy, flapping in the wind, and I thought she looked beautiful up

195

there on the bridge, in her cotton dress and suntanned legs and Blundstones.' It's like Mum's in a trance. 'I remember that thought so well. That she was having a baby, and that I had had a baby too, and it had been difficult, but now I was pregnant again, too early to tell everyone yet . . . and how precious and what a miracle it is to carry a baby. It started to rain. Splatters on the windscreen. Circles. Then there was a . . . a . . . I saw something flash, her golden dress against the black cloud, and there was a thump, and she'd fallen, right in front of my car. I jammed on the brakes, I swerved, but I couldn't avoid . . . her. Another car hit mine from behind. We all stopped. I was shaking so much I couldn't undo my seatbelt.'

She turns to me. 'You were crying in the back, I thought you'd been hurt. I got out of the car, I fell straight over, my legs gave way. Someone called the police. They took the girl away in an ambulance.' She pauses. 'There was an investigation . . . I think the police assumed that she jumped. But she didn't, she was trying to write her message. She slipped, she fell. She was leaning over, to write upside down on the concrete so it would be the right way up for people driving underneath on the road.' Mum is crying again. 'She might not have ever done that before! It had always been the banner tied on, painted on an old bedsheet . . . about the forest.' Mum looks up like she's only now remembering something else. 'She was only eighteen, someone told me that later.' Mum's rubbing her shoulder, the one that gets sore whenever the temperature drops. 'They were hoping to save the baby. I had the windows down. It was raining but it was hot, it was summer, the end of January. Have I already said that?' She stops, swallows. 'It was an accident.'

Mum's looking across at Reed, tears streaming down her face. 'She was your mother.'

I lost that baby. It was the shock.

16

FATHOM

An hour later, Mum and I are sitting downstairs in the hospital café.

Reed is with Mercy and his parents.

'I knew you received the email,' I say. 'From Reed.'

'Liss, I'm so sorry I wasn't honest with you.'

'About a few things, actually,' I say. I don't think I feel angry with her, more shock. And a kind of exhaustion. Just, numb. A sense that I don't really know my mother, or anything, anymore.

'Do you know how Reed found me?' Mum asks.

'Your old email to them was on a usb with some adoption forms. And he googled your name and got the Move Australia website, our street address is on it, for your private clients.'

Mum nods, frowning. 'Probably shouldn't have our address on it.'

The waitress brings Mum a long black and me a hot chocolate.

It's after six-thirty, and Mum usually has no coffee after four, but right now no real-life rules apply.

'They never responded to that email,' Mum says. She plays with a spoon in her coffee. 'It was amazing that Reed survived.'

'How did you know that he did?'

'I rang the hospital. They said it was a miracle. She was only thirty-one weeks pregnant, and the trauma to the baby . . .'

Mum's voice trails off, she sips her hot coffee. Winces. 'I miscarried two days later.'

And just like that, the three pregnancies fall into place, like pieces in a game of Tetris.

She holds my hand. 'I know we should have told you about the donor before now. And it's not fair that you got pulled into all this, and had to, I don't know, resolve all this for me.'

'Who else knows about the donor?' I ask her. 'Does Harry know?'

'Only Dad, me and Jo. Dad may have told Wendy, I'm not sure.'

'Were you ever going to tell me?'

'So many times we almost did, I almost did. We wanted to tell you together.'

'But would you have ever told me?'

'Yes, Liss, I truly believe that we would have.'

I redo my ponytail because it's almost fallen out completely. It's hard to look at Mum. How can I believe anything she says now? Anything either of my parents says? Ever again?

'What about that accident? Who else knows about that?' I ask.

'Dad.'

'Nanna?'

Mum nods. 'Nanna knew. About you, as well.' Nanna died four years ago.

'Does Troy know?'

Mum shakes her head.

'Why didn't you ever tell anyone else?'

Mum finishes her coffee. 'I'm getting another one,' she says, hopping up, 'do you want anything more? Anything to eat?'

'No, thanks.' It's dinnertime but like Mum and the coffee, normal things, like eating dinner, don't seem part of the world I'm in right now.

She comes back from the counter, sits down. 'I didn't tell anyone else, because . . . who do you tell that you accidentally killed someone?'

Now she's asking questions like Reed does. 'I don't know,' I say. I really don't know!

The waitress brings Mum's second coffee. My hot chocolate is getting cold. I realise I have a headache. 'Not your children,' says Mum. 'And not someone you're just getting to know, someone you want to like you.'

That makes Mum sound like she's my age. *Someone you want to like you.*

I finish my drink, scrape the last bits of chocolate out with a teaspoon. 'Did you go to her funeral?'

'I wanted to, but your father told me that was silly.' Mum looks off past the fake plants and speaks almost to herself. 'I was alone. I felt so guilty.' Then she snaps out of her trance. 'You need to know, Liss. There was nothing I could have done differently.'

'I know that, Mum, I understand.'

But she's not listening to me. 'I mean, it wasn't as if I'd been drinking, or speeding. I couldn't have stopped.'

'Mum, I get that –'

'For years I wondered that if my car hadn't hit her, would she have survived the fall? Was it the fall that killed her, or my car? Nobody blamed me. But still, I took a mother from her child. It wasn't my fault, but I couldn't help feeling responsible. Also for the –' she looks down, can hardly say it, 'the baby I was carrying.'

I'm trying to think of the right words. To help this make sense. Seem reasonable. But that's the thing, there's no reason for it. It's like a story with no resolution, no meaning, no moral. What's the moral of this story?

'His mother was so young,' says Mum. 'Only a year older than Harry is now. You know what I never got out of my head? She was only a child herself, but I remember someone from Foster Families telling me that she'd set up a little room for the baby. Apparently she had no money, I don't know where her parents were, or the baby's father. If they even knew. But she'd found a cot from somewhere, a teddy, blankets, nappies all ready. In some ramshackle place she lived, they said it was in the country, just outside Melbourne.'

I picture our shed, set up like a little den for Reed and Mercy.

'Did you tell the police that she fell, she didn't jump?' I ask.

Mum nods. 'I was so distressed, I thought I made it clear. They called it death by misadventure. But the mercy of it was that the baby survived. Delivered in hospital twenty minutes later. A healthy baby boy.'

And now he's here, with us, with me. Reed.

Mum leans forward over the table. 'Don't get me wrong, Liss, people were understanding. The police said move on with your life, just keep moving. So that's what I did.'

'Did you get counselling?'

'I did have one session, I was offered more. I planned to go, but time just went on. It was so hard to talk about. I felt that people would judge me, might think that if I'd been going slower, I could have braked.'

'But no one drives slowly on a freeway, Mum. I don't think you're allowed to.'

We sit there for a while longer. We're the only ones left. The waitress tells us the café will be closing in five.

'Liss, you'll have a lot of questions,' says Mum, 'about this, and about . . . you.'

She's right. I have so many questions jumbled in my head. Not like a list, but all out of order. Like who was the donor, what do they know about him? How did Dad feel? And then I'm getting answers in my head to questions I've never really asked, like why do I wear glasses, why am I small when the rest of the family isn't, have I ever felt apart from them in other ways? Mum looks sad, she's staring at the clock, a big circular one on the wall. Twenty past seven. When I look at it, I can hear it ticking. But it's like time as I knew it means nothing to me now. I can't believe that it was only this morning that we were having the yum cha.

'I often thought of that child,' says Mum quietly. 'I knew he was a boy. For years he was like a little ghost.'

We get up. I'm stiff and sore in my legs, actually everywhere.

'Sometimes,' says Mum, 'I would dream I had a baby, it wasn't you, or Harry, it was a different baby, and he was very sweet and never cried, even when he was hungry or cold. He never put any demands on me. But in the dream, I felt guilty because I knew I wasn't looking after him properly. I was neglecting him, but he never judged me, he loved me all the same. I loved him, too, but I couldn't get myself to care for him properly. I still have that dream . . . sometimes.'

The waitress is putting up chairs and we head out of the café and back to the main reception of the hospital.

'I've thought of the donor, too, Liss,' says Mum as we walk. 'He's been a presence, too.'

I have no idea what to say to that. I'm not sure what happens next. I want to go upstairs, to Reed and Mercy. 'Can we go and see how Mercy is?' I ask Mum. 'She was really sick.'

'You go, Liss, I better call Harry and let him know where we are. I'll come up in a sec. It's level three, isn't it?'

Oh yeah, Harry needs to know all of this as well. I get in the lift and press 3.

Before the lift doors come together, I look over and see Mum once more as an adult separate from me, but not like a physio, knowing exactly what to do like I see her at work. Not moving. Maybe I'm seeing her as someone else might see her. Attractive, fit for her age, in black lululemons and a pale grey zip-up top. Short hair, Jo calls it 'boyish'. It's an auburn colour. I think it's called cherry. She dyes it now. Sitting alone on a low orange couch in the reception area. She doesn't pick up her phone to call Harry. She's just sitting. What is she thinking? Is she remembering that day? Is she regretting?

Maybe as you get older you start to see your parents like that. As regular adults in the world. Mum's got no lipstick on, she hasn't done her hair, but in a way she looks beautiful. I think I do feel angry, but I also feel my heart go out to her. I almost run over and hug her, but the lift doors are closing.

As the lift goes up, I wonder how well any kid ever knows their parents. All the things your parents don't tell you. All their lives before you, the mistakes they've made, the regrets they have. Stupid things they did when they were young, before everything could be recorded forever on the internet. Their fears for you, for them. What they really, truly believe about you. I'm not sure I want to know everything about my mother, but knowing what I do makes me understand her a bit better. The volunteering, the moving, and maybe even the break-up with Dad. When they broke up I thought it must have been because of me and Harry, like you never think that your parents have a part of their life that you're not the centre of.

I get to Mercy's room. I'm about to knock, but they're having a bit of an argument so I wait outside the door.

'You should have told us about Mercy.' It's Reed's dad.

'You should have told me about me.'

Silence. It's a good point, they don't seem to have an answer to that.

'You were such a happy little boy, we didn't want to disrupt you,' says Reed's mother, 'and then when Eliot became so challenging, we didn't want to disrupt things further. He was so difficult and you were so good, and we didn't want to make it harder for you, for us.'

Kids have part of their lives that's separate, too. Like Reed kept Mercy a secret from them. The actual existence of another human being.

I hear Reed's mum again. 'Mercy,' she says. 'Little Mercy. When do you think we'll be able to hold her? You poor little thing, what a start you've had.'

I go in, just as she begins to cry. 'I'm not ready to be a grandmother!' Then the cry kind of turns to a laugh as she leans over Mercy's plastic crib. 'I'm only forty-nine!'

Later, the parents are in the area outside Mercy's room. Reed's mum brought him a change of clothes, so he's had a shower at the hospital. 'That must feel better,' I say.

'So much better!' says Reed. 'And also to lose that hoodie of Eliot's. It was too big.'

We sit by Mercy's crib in ICU, watching her sleeping with the drip going into her tiny arm which is strapped to the base of the crib, her little hand all clean now, nails clean and everything.

'The doctors are waiting for blood test results. Babies can die from whooping cough,' Reed tells me.

'Yeah, I know.' Please, Mercy, I wish in my head. Please be okay. Please, someone, make everything okay.

'And she has an upset tummy because of the cow's milk and the unsterilised water.'

'And probably the banana,' I add, feeling guilty.

Reed nods. 'She was always cold. Too cold for a baby. And malnourished, you know how we thought she wasn't chubby like other babies?'

'Yeah.'

'I thought I was being responsible,' Reed finishes his diagnosis sadly, 'but I wasn't.'

'You were, really,' I tell him. 'You just didn't know exactly how to look after a baby. And if she's malnourished then that would have been from when she was with Eliot and Sienna, before Eliot made you take her. That's not your fault. We tried, with the milk and the banana and the boiled water. And think of what might have happened to Mercy if you'd left her there with Eliot? On the mattress with the rats and stuff.'

Reed is slumped in his chair. He looks so tired. 'You know what's really strange?' he says, taking off his glasses. 'Sometimes, I used to wonder if *Eliot* was adopted. He's so different from me, and from Mum and Dad. He's the bad kid, the disappointment, and he's their actual kid. And I'm the good one, who doesn't give them grief, and I'm not even theirs. I mean, I'm theirs, but not in the same way that he is. And sometimes they really weren't nice to Eliot. They didn't do much to get him back when he left home. They just . . .' Reed pauses, '. . . kind of . . . gave up on him.'

'But you didn't.'

Reed lets out a little sigh. I think he needed to hear that.

I knew what to say.

He looks out the window to the dark, rainy night. 'Eliot took up all the space in our family,' he says. 'I love him, but I worry about him. When he used to go out, I'd always tell him, please don't get drunk, don't take pills, please don't smoke. I pleaded with him to give up smoking, I was so happy when he did. But then he started again.' He smiles. 'Oh Eliot,' as if Eliot is a naughty three-year-old and Reed is a kindly grandfather.

'Do you get why Eliot is the way he is?' I ask.

'Do you mean, like, troubled?'

'Yeah.'

'Kind of.' Reed pauses. 'It's like he was born to go against the rules, and I was born to go with them.'

Mercy is moving in her crib. She's making those cute noises again, but she looks quite peaceful and her breathing seems more even now.

'It's funny,' says Reed, 'because he's six years older than me, and whenever we were out somewhere, our parents used to say to him, "Look after Reed, look after your little brother." And he used to hold my hand and everything, but the whole time, even when I was like five and he was eleven, I felt as if it was me looking after him. He was the one who needed looking after. No one pointed that out to me. I just knew.' He reaches in and touches Mercy's little hand. 'It's weird when you've known someone your whole life, like from when you were born.' He lays his hand on her chest, 'Like with Eliot, the way he is, I can't always understand it . . . but I can feel it.'

'That's a bit like me and Harry, too. But that's funny what you say about thinking Eliot might be adopted. Sometimes I think I'm closer to my dad than Harry is, and now it turns out, well, I need to explain it to you.'

'Yeah, what did you mean when you said you weren't who you thought you were?'

I tell Reed the whole story.

That in trying to discover something about him, I've discovered something about me.

This perfect baby, who brought life back to me,
and to Fiona after all we'd been through.
She felt so much mine,
I wanted to believe
that she was mine.

I adored her,
adore her.

17

AUTHORITY

We get home just after nine. Reed and his family are still at the hospital. They're going to stay overnight with Mercy. I've given Reed my number because he's turned his phone on now.

Mum tells Harry everything. About what happened thirteen years ago, and about me being made with a donor, not our dad.

Harry doesn't say much, just nods and says 'shit' a few times. It's a lot to take in. We're all exhausted. After a while, Harry goes to his room. 'I wish I hadn't had to tell him all of that at once,' says Mum. She touches my arm across the kitchen bench. 'You, too.'

I go and knock on his door.

'Harry, are you okay?'

'Come in, Liss.' He's sitting at his desk. 'Yeah.' He smiles. 'Like, shit.'

Can't he say anything else?

Then he does. He asks me, 'Are you okay though?'

'I think so.' I honestly can't find any word to say how I

feel. Is there a word that means realising that everything you believed about your life turns out not to be real?

'Because, like, you're always, like, totally my sister. Totally.' And he stands up and hugs me.

Oh Harry. Totally.

'Thanks, Harry.' I step back. The note is on his desk.

'I found that,' I say. 'The list. I wasn't snooping, it was to do with Reed.'

Harry drops his head.

I hold out my hand, like he's not my big brother but a little boy. 'Come on, why don't we go for a walk.'

He doesn't move. 'It's night, it's cold, and you've only just got home.'

'We can walk and talk, like we used to. Without Mum hearing. Come on, Harry.'

'It's after nine o'clock, it's freezing out there, what do you want to go for a walk for?' says Mum.

'Mum, can we just have some time?'

She can't say no. She gets that we want to talk about what's happened. And she gets the need to move. 'Well, be careful, please. And don't be long. Stick to the main road. Be back by ten.'

We put on our coats and head down the hallway.

'Harry? Are you listening? I said ten,' Mum calls as we leave.

We don't discuss it but we both know we'll head to the rocket park. Like we're kids but not kids anymore.

The park isn't a place for kids after dark, anyway. It might belong to them in the day, but at night it can belong to anyone – people sneaking out drinking, homeless people, people who want to be alone. At night-time it can feel mysterious, the swings moving backwards and forwards, squeaking slightly.

We've called it the rocket park ever since we were little. I realise that even I'm getting too big for everything. Harry is especially. He can stand on the ground and hold the top of the monkey bars. We sit in the rocket, he can hardly fit, we're too big to climb up inside it, but we can sit on the bottom, our knees scrunched up against the metal of the steering wheel that makes the rocket spin around. The rings of the monkey bars ding gently against each other, like an eerie chime. We used to come down here sometimes on summer nights, when we still had our dog Bernie and no one had walked her all day. But we haven't done this for ages.

'I always thought you were closer to Dad than I was,' Harry tells me.

'Yeah . . . Maybe because he had to try extra hard with me. Like it didn't come naturally.'

But it never felt unnatural, to me.

I don't know what else to say. I don't know how to talk about it, even how I feel about it. I feel strange that the people who made Harry loved each other, even if they don't anymore, but the people who made me didn't even know each other, had never loved each other, never even met each other.

'Will that baby be okay?' Harry asks. 'What's her name? Mercy?'

'I hope so . . . And Harry, that's what Amber's mum was calling the police about. The baby. And Reed. Not the Rate Year Eight stuff. She'd seen us down the street, and then he was on the news.'

Harry nods. 'Right . . . so we told Mum about all that stuff with Amber when we didn't need to.'

'Sorry. What could I do? And she would have found out anyway.'

'Not necessarily.'

'Hey, did you hide a bottle of vodka in the shed?' I ask.

'Might have.'

'Lucky Mum didn't find it!'

He shrugs. 'I wouldn't really care if she did.'

'Reed and I had some.'

'You shouldn't be drinking, you're thirteen.'

'Nearly fourteen. Anyway, it was disgusting. We only had like one sip each. We were so cold, I thought it might warm us up.'

'Did you put it back where you found it – underneath those boxes and the drop sheets?'

'Yeah.' I put my hands on the steering wheel, grip it, it's cold. My legs are cold, too, in my jeans. I should have worn trackies.

Suddenly Harry blurts out, 'I know you're nearly fourteen, I know you'll try drinking, I know you know what those pictures are, Liss, it's just that, I dunno, you're my little sister. You'll always be my little sister.'

What? Oh, the pictures guys send. Some guys.

'Why do you even hang around with those guys?' I ask him.

Harry shrugs. 'I saw them all the time because of footy. But I'm not friends with them anymore. I totally avoid them. Them and Sean, that's the reason I want to give up footy. I'm over it.'

His hand on the wheel makes the rocket turn slowly. I feel a bit sick. 'They've sent stuff to me sometimes,' says Harry. 'Airdropped stuff that they know will embarrass me. Girls, and also . . .' He shakes his head. 'Idiots. I've got all my settings on private now.'

A car goes past and the headlights shine in on us like a searchlight.

'They've so dumped you in it with Amber. She's sure either you made that stupid post, or you gave someone else the nude.'

'But I didn't do either. Like I said, the guys could have got that pic off my phone. Or Amber's sent it to other guys as well, and they've put it up. Guys could have asked her to send them a nude.'

'Then why is she blaming you? If she knows she sent it to other guys?' I think about it for a moment. 'She might have sent it to younger guys, like not your friends, but Year Nines – wouldn't they be more likely to rate Year Eight girls . . .'

Harry spins the rocket, we drift sideways like the whole world is shifting. 'As if I would have done it!' he says. 'She knows I wouldn't have! I'm the one who's nicest to her. I even let her sit on my knee at that party, which was, like, excruciating. I didn't push her away or do really off things like some of the others do, like make off gestures. I let her sit there because I felt sorry for her. Even Sean doesn't stick up for her, his own sister, he laughs along with the others behind her back.' Harry shakes his head. 'He's such a dick, that guy. I'm sure he's part of this.'

My bum and legs have gone numb. The steel seat of the rocket is like sitting on an ice block.

'What happened when she sat on your knee?'

'She crapped on about nothing and I agreed with her about nothing.' Harry tries to stretch his leg. 'Can we get out, I'm getting a cramp.'

We go and sit on a seat. It's wooden, not as cold as the metal.

'We'd been drinking, we smuggled beers in our backpacks and drank them outside the party.' Harry frowns, like he's trying to remember every detail. 'Maybe I came across as more friendly than normal, like, less shy?' He pauses. 'But seriously Liss, she just sat on my knee, I just remember laughing a bit with her because she nearly fell off. Nothing else happened.'

'Okay . . .' I didn't know about the drinking. 'Hey, was that party the day before we had the stall at Camberwell market? She was totally flirting with you that day.'

'Yeah, I think the same weekend.'

'And you were like ignoring her. She bought you the donuts at the market, remember?'

Harry's picking up bits of tanbark and trying to chuck them through the rings from where he's sitting. 'All I remember is it was really uncomfortable. But yeah, it was the day after that party I think. And that night, or it could have been the night after, sometime around then, she sent me a pic of her in her bra and undies.'

'Oh god, what? Where's that one?' I'm panicking that this will be the next pic on their stupid Insta post.

'I deleted that one. Straight away. I promise you, I really did.' A piece of tanbark goes through the ring. 'A few days later she sends me the nude. I messaged her and told her to delete my number from her contacts. I told her to never do that again.'

Now I'm chucking the tanbark bits too, but mine don't go through. 'So this was like, a month ago?'

'Yeah, about that.'

'Then the nude goes up on Insta. Rate Year Eight.'

Harry nods. 'And she goes crazy on her Insta saying how terrible I am and then everyone joins the pile-on.'

I rub my arms. I'm wearing my North Face, but I'm still freezing.

'So . . . she's mad at you.'

'Yeah, because she thinks I'm the one who did it!'

'But also because you rejected her.'

'What do you mean I rejected her?'

'She'd probably decided that you were interested in her.'

'Why? She's like thirteen for christ's sake! And she's a pain in the neck.'

'She's fourteen. And she says she likes older guys.'

'Well I don't like younger girls. And even if I did, I don't like her!'

'But you didn't push her away like the others did.'

'I didn't want to treat her like that! What was I supposed to do? I was being polite, I wasn't leading her on or anything. I felt sorry for her! Jesus, why doesn't she go after one of them on social? They're like the worst to her.'

'She'd be too scared.' I look at Harry, with his straight hair, his fringe that flops to the side, his soft face, his big brown eyes.

He shakes his head. 'It's like she thinks that if a guy isn't a total arsehole to her, it must mean he's interested.'

'Yeah, how sad is that.'

An owl flies over.

'Remember the tawny frogmouth that used to come to our garden at night?'

Harry nods.

I wonder if it's the same one. I think they live for a long time. It sits on top of the monkey bars and stares at us sternly as if to say, Well, what are you going to do about this?

'What do we do now?' I say. 'To fix this? All of this?'

Harry shakes his head. 'Take off to the moon and never come back? Remember we used to think that the rocket could do that? Remember the splashdown game?'

I smile. But we're stuck here on earth.

The tawny frogmouth soars just over our heads. I hear its feathery wings moving through the air.

'Want to walk?' says Harry. 'It's freezing.'

We head down to the oval and start a lap.

'Can you talk to the guys? To Sean? Even just to, like, get to the bottom of what happened, what's happening?'

'He seems to hate me, like everyone else.'

We pass the scoreboard. Home. Visitors. The tawny frogmouth has landed on top of it.

We stop, it's so close. Owls have faces like humans.

'What is even happening in our lives?' I say quietly.

'Yeah, sorry, I should be helping you right now.'

I smile at him. 'I don't know how you could.'

'You should talk to Dad.'

'I suppose. What will I even say to him though?'

'I keep thinking about it but I can't believe it,' says Harry. 'How we didn't know.' He shakes his head and starts to walk again. 'And also that a kid was hiding in our shed. What the hell?'

'I can't believe it either,' I say. 'It's like there's been a cyclone or something. Nothing feels like it did a week ago. When we were going to school like normal, you were going to footy –'

'Yeah, even that's changed. Those guys have wrecked footy for me.'

'What do you mean?'

'They're always going on about getting me a girlfriend. Shit-stirring me. They can be pretty off about it. I'm sick of it. I used to love footy.'

I hope Harry can stand up for himself. I never would have thought this before, but maybe Harry gets the wit of the staircase, too.

'Thanks to them all, my life is kind of ruined.'

We walk around the side of the clubrooms, head back towards the play equipment, the scary swings. I'm trying to think of something to say to make Harry feel better.

'That's how you think now, but look how long life is.'

I put my hand on the cold blue metal of the rocket. 'Do you reckon it might blow over? That people will forget about it?' This is the best we can hope for.

Harry shakes his head.

'Should I tell the wellbeing officer at school? We're supposed to report this sort of stuff.'

Harry puts his hand out too, then both hands, and I remember when we were kids, spinning this rocket together, pretending we could go anywhere.

'That would make my life one million times worse.'

Moving helps. Walking, yoga, any kind of exercise.

We think we're like a digital clock, moving forwards through the numbers. Ticking forwards. Not going in a circle, like old analogue clocks.

But it's always a circle.

SUNDAY

18

FORSAKEN

I go to bed at one and wake up at 4 am.

Sunday. I lie there. Make a list in my head. I can't get back to sleep, so I get up and write it down. Now I see that it's two lists. And they're not even lists, more like questions I don't know the answers to.

What do I say to Dad?

Will Mercy get better?

Will Reed and I be friends?

Hana?

How do I help Harry?

Why didn't they tell me?

Who is he?

Does he ever think about who I might be?

Is anyone telling me the truth?

Will anything ever be okay again????

There's that word.

I read that okay is the most used word on the planet. In lots of languages. It could be because, actually, most people do want things to be okay.

Okay can be a noun or a verb. Now that I think about it, okay can also be an adjective, and an adverb.

Words are always circling in my head, the sound they make, their meanings, how they're used in different ways. No one else in my family is like this. They're more sport, more maths and science people. Jo is creative, but with visual things, not words. Words is only me.

When we get up, Mum, Harry and I are all just walking around the house. Each of us is doing that loop where you go over and over something in your head, trying to get it clear enough to file away. But sometimes it's too early to file stuff and it all has to stay in a mess in your brain.

We're on our phones. Sitting down. Standing up. Opening the fridge. Staring inside, as if the fridge is going to have all the answers for us.

Dad calls twice but I don't pick up. Not because I'm angry, I just don't know how to even talk about it. And I think I might cry if I speak to him. It's like everything has been a lie. And I'm so tired. I don't want to talk to anyone. I hear Mum on the phone and I'm pretty sure she's talking to him. Then he texts me.

Please call me when you can. Anytime day or night.
Love you so much Liss, always have always will x

I think of all the things I loved about Dad. What I miss. Little things, like we always used to go to the café together after my netball matches, just me and him. The way he was proud of me, I could feel that. I made a list ages ago, but I look at it in a different way now.

Reed messages me. They're still at the hospital. Mercy needs to stay longer because her breathing is irregular. They might stay in a hotel in Melbourne for a few days, to see Eliot. And Reed says he's going to try to find out more about his birth mother. Who she was, where she lived. I tell him about what's been happening to Harry.

Harry stays in his room on his computer for most of the afternoon. He says he's studying but who knows.

Mum is cleaning the house like a zombie, going through the motions. I should help her, we both should, but we don't. I've also got study to do but as if I can concentrate on that. Mum goes to check on Hana's place on her own, I don't want to go with her. I want to message Hana but I'm too mad with her. Sadie's done an Insta story of her and Amber at Camberwell market. She's wearing the skirt that I helped her choose last time I went there with her.

I look on Amber's Insta. She's put up a story too, about their day at the market. Captions that say Besties, hearts, true friends. Friends 4 Life. I'm probably being paranoid but I decide she's only doing it to make me feel like I have no friends.

We have egg on toast for dinner. We watch the footy. A twilight game. Collingwood versus West Coast. None of us is interested, they're not even our teams, but it's a distraction.

'Have you called Dad?' Mum asks. 'He wants to come over.'

I shake my head. I don't know what to say to him, to either

of them. While we're watching the footy, I see a new post on Rate Year Eight. It's handwriting, a Sharpie on lined paper.

NEW PIC COMING TOMORROW!

Something clenches in my stomach. Oh god, I bet that will be the other pic of Amber, the one in her bra and undies. Harry said he deleted it immediately, but did he? Does someone else have it?

I'm silently trying to work out what I'll say to Amber. 'I have to say something,' I tell Harry later when I show him the post.

'Please don't,' says Harry, 'I told you, it'll only make things worse.'

On Monday, I realise that things actually can't get much worse.

Every bit of a person's hate, or anger, or jealousy can go public now. Be anonymous. Have power.

And no one can afford to make a mistake, not even a small one.

But don't we all make mistakes?

MONDAY

19

TRUTH

Sadie's at the train station. I don't tell her about the donor or anything. I don't trust her. She asks about Reed and the police and I say, 'He went home. He's back with his parents.' Sadie nods, like it was nothing. And moves on to the next thing.

'Did you see there's going to be a new pic today?' she says happily. 'I reckon they'll put it up at like five o'clock, that's the time for maximum likes.'

'I thought you wanted them to take it down?' I say.

'Yeah, I can't believe they still haven't taken that post down. Amber is so upset. I was with her the whole weekend. She's reported it to Instagram. Inappropriate content.'

'Well, Harry can't take it down because he's not part of that group. He doesn't know anything about it. He never sent that nude to –'

'No offence, Lissa, but you don't know what you're talking about.'

*

I see the Year Elevens lining up for their mid-year exams as we walk into school. Looking at them makes me wonder again why Year Eleven and Twelve guys would want to rate Year Eight girls? Wouldn't they be more about rating girls in Year Ten or Eleven? Year Twelve?

Sadie sees Amber and runs over to her, whispering. Amber's glaring at me as I'm putting my bag in my locker. She hates us both. Me and Harry. Me because I hang around with Sadie sometimes, Harry because she thinks he's doing this to her.

Just before the bell goes, Poppy comes over to the lockers with her phone.

'Is there another post on Rate Year Eight?' Sadie asks, like it's a cool new thing on Insta that we all love.

'No, Amber's put up a pic on her story. Of when they were together.'

'They weren't ever together!'

'Amber's got proof. Amber's got screenshots.' It's like a little chorus behind Poppy, her friends all whispering.

I check my phone. 'If it's in her private group then I can't see it.'

Poppy hands me her phone. She's taken a screenshot from the story. It's a photo of Amber sitting on Harry's knee. She's leaning back into him, almost toppling to the side, and he's holding her. They're both smiling.

She's written a caption: *creep*

'She's got ninety likes already,' says Poppy, taking back her phone, 'she told me. And heaps of comments. See?'

I look at the comments. The top one says they can tell by the way Harry looks at people that he's a sleaze. What?

'She said I could repost it.' Poppy's fingers move rapidly, getting it up on her Insta now. 'It's only been, like, twenty minutes, look how many comments there are!' She's finished. Looks so happy with herself. 'Done!'

I look at the pic now on Poppy's Insta. Stare at it. 'This doesn't mean they were together.'

'No offence,' says Sadie, 'but it does.'

'I think so too.' Poppy nods her head as if to say they all know better. 'It's from that party in the clubrooms.' She turns to Sadie. 'The one she told us about,' she whispers knowingly. 'Amber said all the guys were drinking. Look at his hand, like, yuck, it's almost up her shorts. Hey, let's all repost it, get everyone to!'

In the picture, Harry's hand is on Amber's thigh. She's wearing denim shorts, I remember that she'd been to Queensland and still had a tan.

'I mean it's just my personal opinion –' begins Sadie.

'I am sick of your personal opinion!' I shout without thinking. 'She sat on his knee. So what! My brother's got nothing to do with Rate Year Eight, so find out who it is and get *them* to take it down.'

'Amber says Harry sent around that nude. Her brother told her.'

'Just because someone says something doesn't mean it's the truth. You don't own the truth. Stop spreading rumours about my brother!' I yell at them all.

'Omigod,' Poppy whispers, 'what is *wrong* with you?'

'No offence, but –'

'Shut up, Sadie.' I'm so over her never sticking up for me.

Amber's come to Sadie's rescue. 'Leave Sadie alone. She's my friend, she's been my friend since Year Four. She doesn't need you, or want you.'

I look at Sadie.

She just stands there.

Then I wonder, was it Sadie?

'Did you give them that pic, Sadie?'

'What? As if I'd have it.'

Would Sean have really done it? Would a brother do that?

The bell goes. Amber marches off in the direction of the classrooms, her ponytail swinging from side to side.

Sadie stays still for a minute, between us, then follows Amber.

A moment. I feel fury. What is the truth, about anything? What do I even know?

I scream after her. 'I KNOW MY OWN BROTHER!'

And suddenly, there is no wit of the staircase.

This isn't something I've practised or thought through.

I run up to Amber, grab her shoulder.

'Don't touch me,' she shouts.

'Who made that profile? Whoever did it needs to take it down.'

'Omigod IT WAS YOUR BROTHER AND HIS STUPID FRIENDS!'

'They're not his friends,' I say.

'Leave her, Amber,' says Sadie. 'She's crazy. She lies all the time.'

'Do you even *want* it taken down?' I call after them.

Amber stops. She's starting to cry. 'What are you talking about?'

'Yeah,' says Sadie, 'how can you even say that?'

'I can't believe you're so cruel,' Poppy chimes in. 'Look what you've done to Amber now.'

And then before I realise something, I'm already realising it.

'Amber, who made the profile?'

'Some guys!' She's sobbing, and Sadie and Poppy both have their arms around her, like they're competing to see who's the better friend.

'Okay,' I try to calm myself, 'I'm reporting it to the wellbeing officer.'

'You'll get your brother in heaps of trouble,' says Poppy. 'You'll –'

But maybe all the words, all the meanings, the lists, is just me working out what I really want to say.

I turn to Amber. 'You need to take it down.'

'I can't.'

'You can.'

She runs off, crying.

Now I've realised. The truth.

Amber can take it down because it was Amber who put it up.

I think she made the profile and posted that picture herself.

I wag first period. I find Amber down behind the netball court.

'If you don't take it down, I'm telling the wellbeing officer. They'll report it to the police. It's against the law.'

Amber's crouching with her back to me. 'I didn't know this would happen. I didn't know he'd even look at it.'

'Amber, what are you talking about? It's not some game, it's not a parallel universe. He's a real person. He never asked you to send him a nude. He never posted anything! He has done nothing to you.'

Her face is tear stained, her mascara's run. 'He led me on. He flirted with me.'

'Did he?'

'He kissed me! We were basically going out. And then he just ignores me. He totally used me.'

I don't think he would have kissed her, but I'm desperately trying to see it from her point of view. 'Okay, even if he did flirt with you, your revenge is to totally destroy him? Like he was probably just being nice to you. Unlike those other guys who . . . like . . . think you're a . . . don't take you seriously.'

'What am I supposed to do now?' she yells at me as if the whole thing is my fault.

'Take it down.' I kneel down beside her. 'Will you take it down?'

Amber stands up, brushes off bits of hedge from her dress.

'I'm not speaking to you anymore. I'm never speaking to you again.'

'Good,' I say. 'Suits me.'

I get my books from my locker, go to class.

'Lissa, you're twenty minutes late,' says Ms Ritter.

'I'm sorry,' I say, 'it was unavoidable.'

That was quite easy.

At recess, I check.

Rate Year Eight has been deleted. Amber's post, too.

I message Harry to let him know.

He responds.

Thanks.

Me:

Do you want me to report it to the school or anything?

Harry:

I want her to leave me alone.

Then I get another message from him.

She should never do this to anyone else.

And then one more.

you're the best Liss.

The best sister

'Do you know? Can you guess what I'm about to tell you?'

I take a breath. 'Is it that you think you might be gay?'

THREE WEEKS LATER

20

INFINITY

Reed went home. An ambulance took Mercy to Ballarat hospital so she could be near them. She has to have special medicine and supplements so she can put on weight.

Reed and I message every day. We've even got a streak. We want to get to three hundred days. Reed doesn't just take a random shot to keep it going, he photographs things I might be interested in. Like a new word. He sent me a word I didn't know and had to look up. Solastalgia. 'A form of mental distress caused by environmental change. In many cases in reference to global climate change.' It's what Reed has, I reckon.

It's pretty awful at school. The teachers know about what happened with Amber and Harry, I'm not sure how they found out. Poppy might have told her mum, who teaches Year Ten. I keep waiting for a letter home to the parents. But sometimes schools don't want to make things public if it's bad for their reputation.

Amber took the posts down but they're still on other people's sites, Insta stories and stuff. There are screenshots, they'll never go away. And whoever took the photo of Amber on Harry's knee – it must have been one of the guys at football – could always post again whenever he likes.

Hana's apologised. She messaged me two days after it all happened.

> I'm so sorry Bliss I jumped to conclusions. There's a girl here and a guy said awful lies about her on social her parents got involved it was so bad. I didn't think about what I knew about Harry. I didn't form my own opinions. I'm sorry.

Me:

> That's ok

What else could I say? Even good people believe crap posted online. I've probably done it myself. But I won't now.

Still, I don't know if things will ever be the same for me and Hana. I'll have to wait and see.

I wanted Amber to be punished but all Harry wanted was for the post to be taken down. 'But she was so mean,' I tell him, 'she deliberately set out to hurt you, give you a terrible rep with everyone you know.'

He nods. 'But she might have thought I really was keen on her. Maybe I did hurt her, without realising it.'

I think this is pretty generous of Harry. 'You know that's not the truth,' I tell him.

'It might be her understanding of what the truth is, the way she sees it.'

I think of what Ms Ritter, our English teacher, says: that we live in a post-truth world. 'She still shouldn't have created a fake profile and pretended you shared that photo,' I tell Harry. 'That was NOT the truth. Not anyone's truth – hers or yours. That was really horrible, and mean, and deliberate. That was a lie.'

I want Harry and Reed to meet each other. I text this to Reed. And I ask him how Mercy's going.

> I could have been like Mercy.

Then out of the blue he texts:

> My birth mother's name was Melanie.

Oh wow. I say the name, the word, out loud. No hard sounds. No T, no R, no S. Melanie. I imagine a river flowing. Who we are starts way before we're born.

Apart from her name, Reed's parents say they don't know anything about his birth mother, except they think she lived up around Daylesford somewhere. He's not sure if they know more than they're telling him.

Me:

> You're interested in the same things as Melanie.
> Climate change and preserving forests.

Reed:

> My parents don't like my political views.

Me:

> But your birth mother wanted to make the world a better place. You want to do that too. You can do that.

Then I add:

In her honour.

Reed says he's not ready to look for any other family members yet. Also, he says his parents have enough to cope with right now. They were going to place Mercy in foster care, but they've decided to look after her themselves. She'll be living with them, with Reed. Mercy got out of hospital the other day and Reed reckons they were so proud walking her down the street in a new pram.

Reed's googled Wombat State Forest and the protests back in the early 2000s. A group of people lived up there, actually in the forest. In Wikipedia it says they were living an 'alternative lifestyle'. I don't get what that means, but Mum says that the Daylesford area has always been an alternative lifestyle kind of place. Mum doesn't really want to talk about Melanie, though, about any of that. She tries, but I can tell that she'd rather not.

Then Reed messages me a screenshot of an article he found online.

It names a place. Hidden Valley. Pretty vague. Like an address of someone who never wants to be found. I look on Google maps and it comes up. There's a road. Orchard Lane. There's no street view and when I look on satellite it's just trees but I can see a bit of a clearing. I send it to Reed.

Me:

Is that a building in the clearing? They might have lived there.

Reed:

I want to go and see. Come with me?

It's only half an hour from Ballarat, and an hour from Melbourne. Reed doesn't want to ask his parents because he says they get upset and start to argue whenever he mentions any of it.

I tell Mum and Troy about it over dinner.

'Reed really wants to go there,' I say.

Mum doesn't speak.

'I'll take you, if you like. In the Hilux,' says Troy.

'Would you?'

Reed gets the bus across from Ballarat to Daylesford, and we pick him up there. Troy and I leave at nine-thirty on Saturday morning, it's cold and grey as we cross the Westgate Bridge, the ships sit like shadow blocks on the horizon. Reed would know each one, where it had been, where it was going. He could track them with his Ship Finder app.

Reed is standing neatly like a little kid does, waiting in the cold, wearing a green slicker and his backpack over his shoulder at the bus stop. I tell him to get in the front, he'll want to see Troy's GPS systems on the dashboard.

We head back towards Ballan, turn off at Back Settlement Road and then down a dirt track. 'I think this is Orchard Lane,' says Troy. 'Looks like an old orchard on this side.'

'So this is the regular one, and this one's satellite?' Reed asks, looking closely at the GPS.

'That's right, mate. And you've got your topography on this one, too.'

'Dad was in the army so I looked at maps to see where he was. Apps, too, like tracking apps.'

'I like a flat map, a paper map,' says Troy.

'My parents still use them,' says Reed. 'Not that they'd need to. They've lived their whole lives in, like, a one-kilometre radius. Except for Dad sometimes going on a posting.'

'They were born in Ballarat?' Troy asks.

'Yeah,' says Reed, 'then when they got married they bought a house around the corner from where Mum grew up. They still live in that house. They talk all the time about how much Ballarat has changed, but they haven't changed. They still get a map and spread it out on the dining room table if they're going on a trip.'

I look at the blue dot on the GPS screen. With a paper map you can see the road you went on, follow it with your finger. The blue ocean on the right, the mountains on the left, the next town you'll come to, the place you'll stop for lunch.

This track is through cleared land, but there's forest up ahead, the Wombat State Forest. Daylesford used to be called Wombat. Isn't that the best name for a town? Isn't that the best word? It's funny, and friendly and makes you smile. Wombat.

We enter the forest, there are tall gum trees on both sides of us. The track gets narrower. Troy drives slowly. Blackberries and bracken scrape against the ute.

Sun shines through the trees, but the car window is almost too cold to touch. 'What's the temperature?' I ask Troy. I'm sure that's on his dashboard.

'Three degrees. We can light a fire if we need to.'

Lucky we're in the Hilux because it's a very bumpy ride and there are potholes and deep muddy parts of the track where Troy has to criss-cross so the wheels won't spin and get bogged. Traversing, he calls it. A new word.

The track ends at a clearing with gum trees in a circle all around. Bracken and thistles have grown through the grasses.

'Make that two degrees.' Troy points to the dashboard. Clouds have covered part of the sky, making light and shade dance around the clearing.

Troy stops the ute, turns off the engine, and suddenly it's very quiet. I can hear the trees creaking above us. On the other side of the clearing is a wooden house that's leaning so much that it's literally fallen over. 'Let's have a look,' says Troy.

There's no glass in any of the windows, it's like the house is slowly sinking back into the earth. There's wombat poo and maybe kangaroo poo as well. There's no floor anymore, only beams. We walk along them, balancing.

It looks like people have been here, there's an old mattress, and someone must have lit a fire under the brick chimney because it's full of ash. The wind through the trees is making a whistling sound. Then I hear a plane, and Reed tells me we're under a flight path to the Middle East. We look up through the broken, rusty iron roof to the blue, the clouds and the plane moving in and out of sight. Reed hops off the beam and onto the ground, gets out his phone. 'I'll check the app. Got it, it left Tullamarine fifteen minutes ago. Emirates flight 409.'

More clouds have swept over, wispy and grey. The plane disappears, and it feels even colder.

'I wonder if she lived here?' I say. 'Melanie.'

Reed is still studying the sky.

'Could have been their protest that saved this forest,' says Troy.

Out the back of the house, there's a track that leads further into the bush. We wander along it. There are tyre marks from trail bikes and once or twice I think I hear them far off.

'Who does this forest belong to?' Reed asks no one in that way he does.

'I reckon it's national park,' says Troy. 'Wombat State Forest.'

'So we could come here whenever we like?' asks Reed. 'We could come here in the summer, we could even camp.'

I remember how I've missed camping since Dad left.

'You could come too, Troy,' Reed says, 'if you like camping.'

Part of me thinks that it will never happen, but actually it doesn't matter, because walking on this muddy track with Reed right now, I know that he will be the lifetime kind of friend.

Troy goes on ahead of us. We have to walk fast because it's so cold. Reed is skipping over the really wet parts of the track, his arms out for balance, touching down lightly so his runners won't sink too far.

'Do you think you ever knew?' I ask. 'Like, had a feeling? That you were adopted?'

'Not really. Did you, with your dad?'

'I don't think so.' Then I think of what Jo said. 'But Jo told me a funny thing that day when we went for yum cha. She said that once I asked her if Bruce Springsteen was my dad.'

Troy's waiting for us at a big tree that's fallen across the path. We have to climb over it.

Both Reed and Troy smile. 'How old were you?' laughs Troy.
'Like, three.'

They both laugh again.

I did used to love Bruce Springsteen. I don't know how I
even knew about him, but whenever I hear a Bruce song now,
I remember so clearly everything about being three years old.

Reed keeps shaking his head, laughing. 'What's so funny?'
I nudge him. 'Don't laugh at me!'

'You have to admit it's weird for a three-year-old to love
Bruce Springsteen.'

'And why did I ask if he was my dad? When I had a dad
around!' Maybe, when I was very little I really did think that
Bruce Springsteen was my dad. Then one day I realised that he
wasn't, that it was just one of those silly things that kids think
before they understand the world properly. Or did I somehow
feel what Dad always knew? Like, even though I was a little kid,
I'd captured something in the air, sensed it deeply, in a way I
couldn't understand. The wisdom of everything everywhere
around me.

'Hey, maybe your donor is Bruce Springsteen!' says Reed.

I laugh. 'I don't think so! I think they have to be Australian.
And anyway, Bruce would be too old. Maybe the donor is
someone who likes Bruce Springsteen? Like a fan of his music.
I'll have to ask him that if I ever meet him.'

'Will you try to find your donor?'

'Not till I'm eighteen. That's the law. Mum printed out some
stuff for me.' I stop. 'It's funny because you're adopted and I'm
like half adopted.'

'Look!' calls Troy, as two big grey kangaroos bound over the path ahead of us. They're such funny animals, jumping high on their strong legs like that.

I leap over a puddle. 'Your birth grandparents wouldn't be that old,' I tell Reed. 'They might only be a bit older than your parents. They might live in Ballarat! Or around here somewhere. Imagine if you'd walked past them in the street.'

'I might speak to those Jigsaw people, when I'm older, like eighteen, too.'

'I reckon my donor will be a small frame, like me.' I smile at Reed. 'Like us.'

We reach a fork in the track. The three of us stand still, looking out for more kangaroos.

'Do you have any kids?' Reed asks Troy.

'No kids. I always wanted them,' he adds. 'But it didn't work out that way.'

I don't feel we should say anything more, but Reed just asks the next question.

'How come?'

Troy looks down, then starts on the track that branches to the right, and we follow. 'I was with someone for a long time.'

That doesn't really answer Reed's question.

'Her name was Misha.'

'Didn't Misha want to have children?'

'She did, but she wasn't well enough. It would have been irresponsible.'

I'm not sure what Troy means by that.

'Where is she now?'

'I don't have contact with her anymore,' he says.

So Troy has his own past. Even though he seems to look at things in a straightforward, simple way, says it's easy to be well, his life has still been complicated. It's like everyone has a hidden history.

Troy looks a bit sad as he walks in his strong boots. I wonder if my mum knows about Troy's past, now that he knows about hers. I know she told Harry first, and then she told Troy.

He kicks at something on the ground, for a moment he looks like a teenager. 'We shouldn't regret anything,' he says. 'No regrets.' Troy looks up at the tall trees, their tops swaying in the sky.

We keep walking, and I'm thinking, But isn't it okay to regret? Like we're probably all going to regret something? 'To look back with distress or sorrowful longing; to grieve for on remembering'. That's the definition.

We reach another fallen tree. 'Who's hungry?' says Troy. 'Ready to go back?'

We walk back to what's left of the house. Reed and I have the same stride, take the same size steps. I feel like we're almost twins, like we came together that terrible afternoon on the freeway, me in the back of the car, him in his mother's tummy.

The ground is too wet and so is all the wood around so we can't light a fire, but we have a tarp and a rug and we sit on the broken verandah and hang our legs over the edge. Troy gives Reed an old black jacket from the Hilux because Reed is shivering and it's getting even colder now. We eat the rolls that Troy made, and Reed's mum made scones with sultanas in them. I have to take my gloves off and my hands are freezing.

I can't feel the ends of my fingers, they've turned white. Troy's got a thermos of coffee. I don't drink coffee, but I pour some and hold the warm cup against my hands to stop the numbness.

Troy jumps off the steps and walks around the property, zipping up his puffer jacket against the cold air. There's a couple of other fallen-over buildings, and a shed. He's inspecting each one.

'I wonder what happened to Misha,' I say to Reed.

'She might have died.'

'It didn't sound like it.'

'I reckon we should have a day to remember the dead, and the missing, the missed,' says Reed, hopping down from the verandah. 'Not like ghosts and skeletons, not like Halloween, I mean a day to remember the people we love who have died. I think they have that in other cultures.'

'Yeah, that would be nice,' I say.

It starts to spit, and we move further back under the patches of rotted iron. Drops hit the last bits of roof above us. It's too cold now to stand or sit, we move around to keep warm.

By the doorframe, someone has carved letters. Actually, it's names. A list. Part of the wood has split off so we can only make out some of them.

Ali
Heather
Rayne
Imogen
Will

'Hang on, there are more, here on the other side of the door,' says Reed. 'Do you think it's the people who lived here?'

Mila

Jos

No Melanie. Could Mila be Melanie? Or maybe she was never here.

'These people,' says Reed, stepping back. 'Did they know my birth mother?'

I'm about to tell Reed that this is one of his ridiculous questions, but I'm distracted by the sound of another plane. The clouds are low in the sky and I can't see it, but the sound is clear, this one feels closer. I remember when Reed first talked to me about planes, about all his worries, and 9/11, sitting freezing in the shed with Mercy and the vodka just before I made him leave. It doesn't feel real anymore, but I know it happened.

The grey clouds almost feel like they're touching me. All those people in the sky, texting their families. I shiver. I mean, what would you say? Maybe just three short words . . .

Something makes me look over to the forest. A sound, a movement, another kangaroo maybe, bounding off through the trees. There's another track, a short track to a little clearing, with logs around something stuck in the earth.

I jump down off the verandah. What is it? A post.

Reed follows me over.

It's a small wooden cross. Made by hand.

And then, carved letters in the middle . . .

Melanie Reed

11/11/1987 – 25/1/2006

We love you always

Reed kneels down in the wet leaves and bark, traces each letter with his finger.

The sound of the plane has gone.

Now just the trees. Leaning, creaking . . .

'It's her,' I whisper. 'It's you.'

The spitting rain gets stronger.

'Her name was Reed?' Reed stands up. 'Her surname.' He looks at me. 'What?'

And then the rain is really coming down, heavy and fast and all around us. But we don't move. We stand there as it covers us, tumbling, dripping from the gum trees in the sky, and everything smells cold and of eucalyptus.

Troy is jogging back across the clearing, the hood of his jacket over his head.

'Who wants to go into Daylesford and get a hot chocolate? Let's find an open fire somewhere . . .' He stops.

The rain falls, straight and silver.

Troy puts a hand on Reed's back.

'Looks like you've found her,' he says quietly.

We stand at the edge of the forest, amongst these beautiful ruins of the beginning of Reed's life. And suddenly it goes so quiet, and the fast falling rain seems to switch into slow motion. The whole world slows down, something is floating, gracefully. I look up and it falls upon me – white, feathery, tender. It lands softly on the bracken, the grass, the thistles, the little wooden cross, transforms the whole clearing, it becomes magical.

'Look!' I whisper. It almost takes my breath away.

Snowflakes land on our noses, on Reed's eyelashes, melting immediately. And it's like everything goes from hard and harsh and cold to something like a beautiful, delicate, gentle song.

Reed turns to me. 'See what I mean?' he says.

After a few minutes, Troy and I pack up the rug, the thermos. Reed stays sitting on the log by the little cross, his coat glistens.

I put the stuff in the car. Cold mud has oozed into my runners, my toes are wet.

'Hey, Troy,' calls Reed.

Troy turns, his hood covering half his face. 'What, mate?'

'Thank you for bringing me here.'

We get in the Hilux. 'Now, hot chocolate,' says Troy as he starts the engine, turns on the heater and the demister for the windscreen. I take off my wet shoes and socks, put my feet up against the heating vent between the front and back seats. I look out at the snow falling, the rain turned to snow.

And guess who's on Triple J?

Like, how often would Triple J play Bruce Springsteen?

I love you.

SIX MONTHS LATER

21

SYNCHRONICITY

It's like that moment when you realise once and for all that Father Christmas doesn't exist. That all the adults in the western world have joined together in this huge lie. I mean, it's incredible! Made up, constructed, not true. Post truth.

But this isn't Father Christmas. This is my actual life. Day to day, nothing has changed, but underneath, my life is totally different from the way I understood it. The people I had always trusted weren't the people I thought they were. I am literally a different person.

It's the same for Reed.

He was so confused by the fact that his parents gave him Melanie's surname when they didn't want him to know anything about her. It doesn't make sense. Reed asked his parents about it. His dad wanted to call him Andrew – which is actually his middle name. But his mum wanted Reed. When he asked why, his mum just said, 'That poor young woman, it was the right thing to do for her.' Then she didn't want to talk about it anymore. It's the only time she's ever mentioned Melanie.

I think it was the right thing to do for Reed, too. To give him that name. Which makes me think that sometimes people *want* one thing to happen, like for Reed to never find out, but inside, without even knowing it, they *need* something else to happen. So they give him a way that he might find her.

It's almost Christmas time now, we're having an afternoon thing at our place because Dad and Wendy and the twins are over from Beijing. Dad's holding little Coco and my mum leans across and says, 'He used to hold you in the same way.' At first it almost creeps me out, I can't see myself as a baby against his chest, and what did he even feel, holding me? The same as holding Coco, now? But then I close my eyes and let myself imagine it, being safe and warm in strong arms.

In some ways I wish I was a little child again. It's a strange feeling, like who am I now? Not a child of his anymore, Coco and Clementine's big sister, but not technically their sister at all. Like I'm not biologically related to them. I used to always want a little sister, I'd ask Mum to have one all the time. And the baby Mum lost, it was a donor baby, too. Mum told me. The same donor. They had to let the donor know that the pregnancy was 'not viable'. That's the actual term for it. Mum told me that it was a girl. So I almost had a sister. A real, totally related sister.

Before the others get here, I facetime with Hana. In the morning a pic came up on my Insta feed for one year ago today. Me and Hana in the hammock in our back yard. A selfie. We'd been to the Camberwell market on the train and bought all these outfits. Hana has a cool style, not like anyone else's. I bought a denim skirt that day, with tiny beads sewn into it.

I wore it all last summer. Hana wears long colourful skirts or baggy pants that she finds at the markets. Amber and the others always turned up their noses, but they looked at Hana as if they were trying to work out how she put those outfits together. Not that they'd ever ask her.

She tells me, 'It's been hard making friends here, too. My year level are all older than me. I'm always trying to keep up. I mean it's great but it's harder than I thought. And they all have heaps of money – much more than we do.'

That's because their parents are building the mines and Hana's parents are rejuvenating the land once the mines have wrecked it. They're like on opposite teams. And the team building the mines gets most of the money.

'Hey,' I say, 'I would never have thought you were finding it hard from what you put on social.'

'It's like everyone says,' Hana tells me, 'social's only a highlights package, isn't it?'

Hana has some great news, too. 'We're coming over in the Easter holidays. We reckon there might have been squatters at our place. The neighbours saw someone on the porch, sleeping bags and stuff. Mum wants to have a meeting with the real estate agent about getting a permanent tenant.'

I don't tell Hana that it was Reed. Maybe when I see her, I will. We say goodbye because Jo has arrived and she's talking to me as if I'm not on the phone at all. 'Is that Hana? Say hi from Aunty Jo. Hi Hana, hi darling!' She yells into my phone.

I bought Christmas presents for Coco and Clementine. A first dictionary and a weird alphabet book that actually won't help them learn the alphabet at all. It's called *P is for*

Pterodactyl. Each word starts with a letter that you don't say. Like M is for Mnemonic. W is for Wren. I show Dad before I wrap it up. 'Thanks,' he says, 'this will totally confuse them!' But he looks really happy.

Dad's apologised to me about a million times, and we've talked a lot about what happened. With Mum, too. I was angry because even though he is my dad, like he's the only dad that matters to me, I still have a right to know who I am. Sometimes I think I want to know my donor's name, so I don't have to keep calling him 'the donor'; sometimes I want to see his face . . . I only talk about that stuff with Reed.

Troy's made dips, and flatbread toasted with oil and salt and herbs on it. Mum's bought brownies. Reed's parents are bringing a cake. Coco and Clementine are the cutest little girls, not identical but very alike. Black hair and smiley eyes and round, chubby faces.

When Reed and his parents arrive with Mercy, Mum takes Mercy in her arms. Reed and I really tried with Mercy, but when Mum holds her it looks so normal, so comfortable and confident.

'She's grown,' says Mum. 'And look at her curls!' Mercy's got more hair now.

'She's almost walking,' says Jan proudly.

As if she heard Jan, Mercy pulls herself up so that she's standing, holding on to the edge of the chair, and beams at us all. She looks so healthy, and chubby like a baby should look. She has chubby little arms and hands, now.

My family used to be Mum, Dad, son, daughter. Then it

changed to Mum, son, daughter, Dad, new partner. And now there's a family that looks like this:

Mum – Fiona
Brother – Harry
Dad – Nick
Stepmum – Wendy
Half-sisters that technically are not my blood relatives
– Coco and Clementine
De-facto stepdad (maybe) – Troy
Donor – someone, somewhere

Then there's Reed. Old-fashioned, funny, caring Reed. And Mercy. Wendy says that babies bring their own luck. And it feels good to hold a baby, it's so real and pure – one person holding another person.

And Reed's parents – Jan and Peter. They seem old. I can't believe that Jan is only one year older than my mum. Peter's very formal. They're both quite stern. Serious. The only people I know who go to church. Hard people to talk to, sometimes hard to understand. Reed actually looks quite like them. He said that with adoption, they try to choose parents who look like the baby, so it's easier for everyone.

Harry holds Clementine. He didn't like holding the twins when they were newborns, but he's better at it now. When Harry first held Mercy, he held her out in front of him with his arms straight. 'Not like that!' I said.

Reed tickles Mercy and she giggles. It's the most beautiful sound in the world. A baby's giggle. Joy.

Harry laughs, too. Feels like for the first time in ages. Bella messaged him after the formal, said there had been rumours about him ever since the party in the clubrooms. Bella didn't believe the rumours but she was scared that if she said anything, then Amber and Sean would get people to turn on her.

Heaps of people turned on Harry. For a while, I couldn't see how Harry could move on from there. But he has, and we both avoid Amber. She's found other people to spread rumours about. Harry's nearly eighteen now, he only needs nine more hours for his licence.

Harry was pretty calm throughout the whole thing. Mum used the word 'dignified'. He said Amber must be so insecure to do what she did. Trolling yourself. Like self-harm, but digital. I even found out that the Amy person who said the nude was Amber was just another fake profile Amber made up. She outed herself on that post.

'But you were the victim of it,' I said to Harry.

'I'm not going to be a victim,' he told me.

'She really hurt you,' I said.

'She must be hurt, too,' said Harry.

And that made me think. Hurt is an adjective as well as a verb. Like, hurt people hurt people.

I hope Harry has people to talk to. I think he's making other friends now, not just the guys from the footy club. He's been to some gigs and festivals, seeing bands, with people whose names I haven't heard him mention before.

We go out on the deck. It's sunny, and Mum puts the umbrella up over the table. I think of Reed that first afternoon. Holding Mercy, in the cold. The fright I got when I saw him, standing on our deck looking terrified. It feels like a long time ago.

There are some new meetings at this get-together. Troy hasn't met Dad yet, or Jan and Peter. And Eliot is supposed to come but he hasn't shown up yet. I still haven't met Eliot. Sienna is still in Queensland, I think. I don't know what will happen with her. Reed says that his parents don't talk about it and he doesn't like to bring it up.

But they see Eliot sometimes now. They take Mercy to him and he goes to the park with her. I suppose if your kid really lets you down, then gets into trouble and he needs you, what can you do but take him back?

Troy and Dad are weirdly polite with each other. I see them a bit later, having a beer by the kitchen bench. Troy puts a tray of chicken in the oven and now neither of them have anything to do except stand there with their beers.

'It's only a courtyard out the back, but I've got a few veggies on my nature strip,' Troy's saying. 'People can pick parsley, or some chives, rosemary or whatever. Lots of people walk up my street from the train station.'

Dad nods.

Troy says, 'Not hard to make something where we are.'

Oh Troy.

Dad doesn't know what to say, but Reed is nodding enthusiastically, so impressed that Troy is using public land to grow food. I actually feel really emotional. I don't know where to look. So I look at Dad, at Reed, at Troy, we look to each other.

Suddenly Reed says, 'You know Troy won a medal? For rescuing people in the surf.'

'Are you actually Jesus Christ?' laughs Jo. 'Come on, Troy, you must have some vices.'

'Don't worry, I do.' Troy smiles.

He puts his arm around Reed. 'I reckon you deserve a medal, too, mate.'

I look around, and I wonder who we might add to this odd mix of people. Maybe the person who helped me become alive, gave me life? Maybe Eliot, I hope he'll come. Jan keeps looking towards the door, then at her watch. Peter says to her, 'Relax, it doesn't matter, let's just enjoy the day.'

For the moment, this is enough.

I don't believe a family is only about genetics. I found a new word in the dictionary. Framily. It's a portmanteau word, like blog, and brunch, and labradoodle. A blend of friend and family. I've got the definition in my phone. 'A group of people who are not related by blood but who constitute an intimate network and a sense of belonging.'

Jo opens a bottle of champagne. 'Jan and Peter don't drink alcohol,' says Mum quietly.

'What, not even a sip at Christmas time?' Jo almost shouts. 'A mineral water then? Ice? Lime? Cheers, everyone!'

Jan looks quite startled. People react to Jo in this way but she never seems to pick up on it.

Jan goes to heat up Mercy's bottle. Peter is inside with Dad and Troy. Harry's there, too, holding one baby and Dad's holding the other one. So it's just me, Mum, Jo and Reed at the table outside.

I've noticed a change in Mum. Like just sitting here now, normally she'd jump up to get something, do something.

She's going up to Ballarat one day a fortnight to look after Mercy – she says to give Jan and Peter a break. Probably the volunteering job that she was always searching for.

Jo takes a swig of champagne, sits back in the sun. 'Even though you caused a lot of trouble, young Reed, it's turned out well that you ran away with Mercy.'

Reed is checking cricket scores but he puts his phone down. 'When I think about it, it was so stupid, I'm not even sure what I wanted.'

He turns to me. 'What did I even want?'

I smile. Still with the questions I can't answer.

Jo hurls an olive pip into the garden, and at last someone has an answer to one of Reed's questions. 'My theory is that you wanted your birth mother back. That the end of your little adventure was that you were going to discover her.'

Reed nods slowly. 'Then I discovered that she's never coming back.'

'True,' says Jo, and now even she seems a bit lost for words. She cuts a chunk of cheese, puts it on a cracker with some quince paste.

'I can be here.' Mum opens her hands. 'We can all be here.' She picks up the plate of brownies, offers them to Reed. 'I wanted that baby to know that I thought about him, I cared.'

Reed puts his brownie neatly on the table. 'I know.' He stands up as if he's about to make a little speech. 'Thank you for giving me that opportunity.'

Mum looks at Reed as if no one else is at the table. 'I wanted to be forgiven.'

Reed sits down again, puts his brownie on a plate. 'I think people need to forgive themselves, too.'

I feel his smooth, warm skin beside me, this magical brother whose arrival triggered everything – about Mum's past, and Troy, and me, and Dad and Wendy. I can't help thinking that Reed was sent from some kind of force in the world. That when we both needed each other, we were there. Neither of us knowing who we were, his discovery leading to mine . . . It makes no sense at all, it's like Bruce Springsteen coming on Troy's car radio just after we'd been talking about him. There's a word for that. Synchronicity. I like that word. I might put it on my list.

Late in the afternoon, Reed and I are sitting on the grass with Mercy. I'm getting better with babies. I actually find them fascinating. I could watch Coco and Clementine, play with them, for hours. It will be fun when they all start talking.

Reed is so relaxed with Mercy now, he's like a little dad. And she adores him! She calls him Dee because she can't say Reed. It's very cute. It was her first word. When he's near her and she holds out her arms to him, he rolls his eyes like he's saying Oh Mercy, leave me alone, but you can tell that he loves it.

Mercy likes to stand on her wobbly little legs and hold our hands so we can steady her. We're trying to get her to take a step, between us on the grass.

Lissa is a quick name. But with Reed, there's a long way between the R and the D. You can't say it quickly. You have to pause on the eeeee sound.

People think we grow up evenly each year. But we don't. I've done a heap of growing up in the last six months. And in those few days. Back then.

We all have.

Mercy, too. Because now, Reed lets go of her hands and she takes a step.

Then another one.

'Mercy!' Reed cries, reaching out for her, 'You did it!'

And he turns to me and smiles, like with his eyes, his whole face, like a baby smiles, like Mercy, and that's when I know everything is going to be okay.

Things I've learnt about people

> *Harry is strong*
> *Troy is kind*
> *Mum is forgiven*
> *Amber is sad*
> *Sadie is weak*
> *Hana is human*
> *Reed is brave*
> *Eliot is loved*
> *Mercy is saved*
> *I belong*
> *We all belong*

FIVE YEARS LATER

'You like him too? Which song's your favourite?'

'"Born to Run". Which one's yours?'

'"Growin' Up".'

ACKNOWLEDGEMENTS

Thanks to Jeanmarie Morosin, Karen Ward and everyone at Hachette. And to Allison Colpoys for creating a beautiful cover in time she didn't really have. To Deonie Fiford for her sensitive and thoughtful copyedit. I am very grateful to each of you.

Thanks to my agent, Pippa Masson, for her ongoing support.

Thanks to Caroline Williams who shared her story, and Paddy's story, with me.

And to Patrick Verdon who shared his dream in which he heard the line 'hurt people hurt people'.

Thanks to Ella, Tom, Lucy, Joe, Sophie, Angus and Lulu for their insights, and for the many conversations we had about social media culture. Thanks in particular to Sasha Whitehead for her support, interest and helpful feedback at the eleventh hour.

Thanks always to Michael, Wil, Lizzie and Mitch.

Jane Godwin is the highly acclaimed and internationally published author of many books for children and young people, across all styles and ages. Children's Publisher at Penguin Books Australia for many years, Jane was the co-creator with Davina Bell of the Our Australian Girl series of quality historical fiction for middle readers. Jane's books include her novels *Falling from Grace* and *As Happy as Here* (a CBCA Notable Book 2020), and picture books *Go Go and the Silver Shoes* (illustrated by Anna Walker), *The Silver Sea* (with Alison Lester and patients at the Royal Children's Hospital, Melbourne) and *Watch This!* (with designer Beci Orpin and photographer Hilary Walker). Jane is dedicated to pursuing quality and enriching reading and writing experiences for young people, and spends as much time as she can working with them in schools and communities and running literature and writing programs.

janegodwin.com.au
@janiegodwin